not quite
the perfect
boyfriend

D0958668

not quite
the perfect
boyfriend

Lili Wilkinson

ALLEN&UNWIN

This edition published in 2011
First published in 2008

**Allen & Unwin**
83 Alexander Street
Crows Nest NSW 2065
Australia
*Phone*  (612) 8425 0100
*Fax*     (612) 9906 2218
*Email*  info@allenandunwin.com
*Web*    www.allenandunwin.com

ISBN 978 1 74237 765 0

Cover photo: Heidi Schawel/Workbook Stock (RM)/Jupiterimages
Design based on cover design by Tabitha King and Bruno Herfst
Text design by Bruno Herfst
Set in 12.5/16 pt Spectrum MT by Midland Typesetters, Australia
Printed in China at Everbest Printing Co.

10 9 8 7 6 5 4 3 2 1

# pro·nun·ci·a·tion key

ə  as in *allow me to
    humiliate myself*
ɛ  as in *extremely strange*
i  as in *eek!*
æ  as in *at least I can
    still spell*
ɪ  as in *intelligent*
ɒ  as in *on a scale of
    one to ten*
eɪ  as in *atypical*
ʌ  as in *ugly*
u  as in *school*
ɜ  as in *hurt*
b  as in *biscuits*
k  as in *Care Bear*
m  as in *MySpace*

n  as in *nice arms*
s  as in *secrets*
t  as in *trying too hard*
p  as in *project*
r  as in *revenge*
v  as in *vomit*
l  as in *lavender bushes*
g  as in *gross*
h  as in *harlot*
z  as in *zillion*
w  as in *wizard*
f  as in *fake*
θ  as in *think*
ʃ  as in *shame*
dʒ  as in *joust*
ʒ  as in *closure*

# 1  com·mence·ment

/kəˈmɛnsmənt/

–noun; an act or instance of commencing; beginning.

– A Wordsmith's Dictionary of Hard-to-spell Words

Sometimes I wish I could just grow down and go back to primary school. Everything was easy then. School was fun, I was the Grade 6 Spelling Champion, and my best friend and I thought boys were disgusting.

When I wake up on the first day of Year 10, I realise how much has changed. School is hard. My best friend is boy-crazy. I have never kissed a boy. And no one gives a rat's fundament about spelling.

I drag myself into the kitchen for breakfast. Mum and Dad are talking, but stop when I come in. Mum looks down into her cup of tea, and Dad leaves the room.

'Is everything okay?' I ask as I eat last night's ravioli straight from the Tupperware container.

'Fine,' says Mum, then makes a face. 'Imogen, that's disgusting.'

Mum named me Imogen because it sounded like

*imagine*, but everyone calls me Midge. Even Mum only calls me Imogen when I'm doing something wrong.

I pop another piece of ravioli into my mouth. 'What?'

'You could at least heat it up.'

'I like it cold.'

Mum empties the dregs of her tea into the sink and then smoothes her shirt. She was a total hippie before I was born, but now she works for a classy law firm in the city. She still burns incense and talks about karma, and she gets all hot under her Country Road collar when I call her a sell-out.

I finish the ravioli, and rummage through the fridge to find something worthy of a sandwich for school.

'Don't bother making your lunch,' says Mum, gathering up the official-looking papers that decorate the kitchen table. 'I'll give you money to buy something.'

I freeze. 'What have you done with my mother?' I ask suspiciously.

'It's your first day back at school,' says Mum. 'You should have a treat.'

I raise my eyebrows. 'This from the woman who started a letter-writing campaign to our local council insisting they serve tofu in the school canteen.'

She just smiles and snaps her briefcase closed.

Tahni bounces up to me at my locker in the Year 10 corridor. She's been in Queensland with her family since after Christmas, so I haven't seen her in forever.

We squeal and hug and do the girl thing, then she

launches into a lurid and, I suspect, highly exaggerated description of the boys she met on the beach, and the bikini she wore, and the expressions on the faces of the boys when they saw her in the bikini, and the photo she gave them of her in the bikini (airbrushed, of course – Tahni became a Photoshop expert last year with the sole purpose of being able to airbrush her own photos). I zone out after a couple of seconds. I notice a sign on the wall:

**"Welcome" Year Ten's**

I can forgive Tahni her tendency to turn even the most mundane events into a drama worthy of Ramsay Street, but there are only two things worse than poor spelling. One is misplaced quotation marks. The other is unnecessary apostrophes.

'So?' asks Tahni. 'Did you meet any hot boys over the summer?'

She says it in this annoying sing-song voice which makes me blush. Because she knows the truth. She knows I've never kissed a boy. She's the one who tells me at every available opportunity that I'm going to be a lonely old lady with eleven cats in a caravan.

I feel like the whole school is judging me. Me in all my pathetic loser-y glory.

This is an extra-special bonus level of Not Fair. It's not like I'm ugly. I've spent hours in front of the mirror, trying to figure out what is wrong. I have good skin. My eyebrows are nicely shaped. I don't have crooked teeth or a hideous squint. So. What. Is. The. Problem??

Tahni laughs and makes miaowing noises. I envisage a whole year of this. A whole year of every girl in the school who isn't me pashing anything with a Y chromosome. And I can't handle it. I would rather die.

So I say it. I don't think about it. I just say it.

'I did meet a boy.'

Tahni giggles. 'Cousins don't count, Midge,' she says. 'Or pizza delivery boys. Or the boys who work at the video shop.'

I glare at her. 'I met him at the library,' I say. 'He has wavy brown hair, and he's English.'

I pause. What am I talking about? I didn't meet any boys.

'So he's a nerd,' says Tahni, cautiously.

Does that mean she bought it?

I grin. 'A hotty Mc-Hot nerd.'

Tahni nods appreciatively.

Who doesn't love a hot nerd?

'Wow,' she says. 'You really met a boy. When can I meet him?'

'He's gone back to England,' I say. Where is this all coming from?

'So you'll never see him again,' Tahni says dismissively, like it doesn't count.

'He might be moving here.'

What am I doing? I'm crazy. There's no way Tahni will buy this.

But she is. She's leaning forward, her eyes intent.

'Did you pash him?'

'Of course.'

Tahni lets out a little squeak of excitement. 'Are you off your V-plates?'

I give her a Look. 'Don't be gross,' I say. 'We only met a month ago.'

'So what did you do?' asks Tahni. She looks slightly defensive. Maybe she's worried that I have a better story than her never-ending Bikini on the Beach masterpiece. I'm enjoying this way more than I should.

'We went on a picnic by the river,' I say. 'We had a picnic rug and lemonade and dip and squishy cheese. He made me a garland out of daisies and willow branches and called me a princess.'

Tahni frowns, and I know I've gone too far. 'Sounds kind of wet,' she says.

'It wasn't,' I say. 'It was romantic.'

The bell rings. 'More on this later,' says Tahni over her shoulder as she hurries off to form assembly.

I am officially insane.

## 2  thes·pi·an

/ˈθɛspiən/

–adjective; pertaining to tragedy or to the dramatic
  arts in general.

– A Wordsmith's Dictionary of Hard-to-spell Words

When I found out Tahni and I were in different home
groups, I was furious. How could they split us up? Tahni
and I have been best friends since Grade 2, when we bonded
over a shared love of pineapple jelly-snakes, and a shared
hatred of Nina Kennan, the school's resident Little Miss
Perfect.

Now, as I slip into form assembly alone, I'm just relieved
to be away from the boy-interrogation.

What on earth was I thinking?

When I was a kid I had an imaginary friend called Susan,
who had curly red hair and could tap-dance. Dad thought
it was cute. Mum thought it was an expression of my inner
creativity, or possibly a shadow of a past life. I think she was
secretly hoping that my imaginary friend would be
Aboriginal, or Cambodian, or someone Spiritual and Ethnic
with feathers in their hair who could talk to animals and

was called Runs With Bears. But no. The closest Susan ever got to being Spiritual or Ethnic was the all-singing, all-dancing concerts that she and I staged together. I blame my grandmother, who took me to see *Annie* when I was five.

Dad was right. Imaginary friends *are* cute. Redheaded, tap-dancing ones especially so. When you're *five*. When you're sixteen, it's not so cute. When you're sixteen, it's deranged. I should see a doctor.

At the front of the room, Ms Church clears her throat, and slowly, everyone sits at a desk and stops discussing the relative merits of spray-on-tan versus solarium tanning (is it better to be messy and orange, or to risk getting cancer and looking like a handbag by the time you're thirty-five?). I hadn't even noticed Ms Church entering the room. She's so tiny I seriously think she could apply for a disability pension. I had her for French last year, which would have been fine if the poor woman could actually speak French. All I had to do was make lots of French-sounding, throat-clearing noises, and I got As.

'Imogen Arkles?'

I jump. Ms Church may be the size of a malnourished hobbit, but she sure can project. She's got a voice like a seagull. A seagull with a megaphone.

'Here.'

I'm almost always first on the roll. It sucks because I can't slip into form assembly that precious extra twenty seconds late, like Joe Wilson or Shuchun Zhao.

It does have its benefits though, because once I've done my 'here' duty, I can zone out and think about more important matters (like what to get for lunch with the ten dollars Mum gave me), while all those familiar names go washing past (or, in Ms Church's case, screeching past).

I'm wondering whether a meat pie or a sausage roll has more calories, when I notice Ms Church's constant nails-on-blackboard squeal has stopped. I pop back into reality, just in time to be blasted again.

'George Papadopoulos?'

Everyone is looking around. A new name. We're getting a new kid? A *boy*?

The girls all sit up a little straighter, apply lip gloss and smooth or mess up their hair, depending on whether they are the smooth kind or the messy kind. I find myself sitting up a little straighter too.

A new boy.

I imagine him walking through the classroom door.

*He's tall and gorgeous. His soft brown eyes zoom straight to me, and we have a Moment. Ms Church has to clear her throat, and the New Boy blushes and looks away. But that Moment is all we need to know that we are Meant To Be Together.*

I'd have to break up with my English boyfriend first, of course. But he's gone home anyway, and everybody knows that the long-distance thing doesn't work.

Okay. I am seriously insane. I am feeling guilty about breaking up with my PRETEND boyfriend in order to get it on with a new PRETEND boyfriend. Le sigh.

Ms Church shrugs and moves on down the roll to Cherry Pham.

But then we hear footsteps in the hallway, and the door opens, and he's there. The New Boy.

He isn't tall. He also isn't gorgeous. About the only thing I got right is the brown eyes.

He's sort of . . . lumpy. Not fat, but he could lose a few kilos. He has dark brown hair that is too long to be normal, and too short to be skater/surfie cool. It's curly in a kind of girly way, and is in desperate need of some Product.

And he's wearing the Official School Shorts, which no one wears. Seriously, no one. Not even the boys who spend their lunchtimes in the library playing chess. (Not that there's anything wrong with that. As the Grade 6 Spelling Champion, I understand the vilification that comes with being committed to a Cerebral Extra-Curricular Activity. I'm sure those chess-boys in the library are lovely, well-adjusted young men. But, you know, if anyone was going to be wearing the Official School Shorts, it would be them. And they don't.)

It actually looks like his mother may have dressed him. All the other boys wear their uniforms in a slouchy, grubby, who-gives-a-rats kind of way. Their shirts are rumpled, their ties half undone and all skewed. Their oversized grey pants hang so low that their boxer shorts show. (What is *with* that? And how do they do it without, you know, *hips*? Do they have some kind of complicated pulley-suspension thing to stop their pants from falling down? Maybe this is why I don't have a boyfriend. Because I can't appreciate the scientific and aesthetic skill that goes into wearing your pants around your knees.)

The New Guy's uniform fits. It's clean and freshly ironed. His top shirt button is done up, with the tie knotted neatly over it (a half-Windsor, by the look of it). He actually has his shirt *tucked in*. He's lucky we aren't in Year 7 anymore, or he would probably be beaten up for coming to school dressed like that. Now we're All Grown Up and in Year 10, the other boys will just ignore him, make crude jokes about his mother and possibly pay him to do their homework.

'George Papadopoulos?' screeches Ms Church.

The New Boy nods. Ms Church makes a note on the roll.

'Take a seat,' she says. 'And please try to be on time in the future.'


I have English, Twentieth-Century History and Maths before recess. In each class, the teacher hands out the course outline, tells us that they won't go over it in detail because we can hopefully all read by now, and then stands up the front of the class and reads the entire thing out, word for word. The only variation is in History, where Mr Loriot speaks to a PowerPoint presentation.

I count three spelling mistakes in the English outline (*consistant, recieve* and *reccommend*), and a typo (*assingment*) and a misplaced apostrophe (*integer's*) in Maths. History has no mistakes that I notice, but Mr Loriot loses points anyway for having one of those PowerPoint presentations where every single font/colour/transition/background/noise is used to create optimum irritation and confusion.

I'm so completely brain dead after two and a half hours of 'assessment criteria' and 'submission requirements' that when the bell goes, I zombie-walk out of class to my locker without even thinking about what is awaiting me.

Ambush.

Tahni is practically drooling with anticipation. I don't even have time to open my locker and put away my new grammatically inaccurate course outlines before she launches the first strike.

'When is he moving here? What colour are his eyes? Did you pash on the first date? If there was a movie about you guys, who would play him?'

I can't tell if she's genuinely interested, or if she's trying to catch me out.

I try to kick-start my brain back into action. 'Um. I don't know. Blue. No, but we held hands. Um, an English Zac Efron?'

Tahni drags me to the canteen. I am so flustered that I order a vanilla slice instead of hedgehog. I am frogmarched off to a shady corner, where I am further interrogated.

During recess, I tell her that my boyfriend lives in Surrey (I don't even know where that is, but it sounds sufficiently hedges-and-high-tea), is an only child like me and loves watching re-runs of M*A*S*H. He listens to This Broken Tree, but he isn't emo and he's also into The Beatles. He is right-handed. He is a Libran. He reads the classics (Dickens, not the Brontës), biographies (the Dalai Lama and Barack Obama), literary fiction (Gabriel Garcia Marquez) and graphic novels, but not comic books. He plays lacrosse.

When the bell rings for the end of recess, I gratefully drag my exhausted brain back to class, where I sit through another two mind-numbing periods of course outlines (Psychology: *cognative*. Politics: *election's, govermnent, standerd, the five living prime minister's* and *upholding 'democracy' in Australia*). I have no classes with Tahni – she's doing vegie-maths and as many IT subjects as she can. It turns out that she's good at computery things other than airbrushing. She says she wants to do Digital Design and Communication at uni when we finish. I reckon that first she needs to learn that there are two 'm's in *Communication*, but that might just be because I'm jealous. I have no idea what I want to do after school. Can you do a Bachelor of Spelling? Or a Diploma of How to Look After Your Eleven Cats in a Caravan?

The new guy – George Papadopoulos – is in my Politics class. He is also in my English class. I sit behind him in Politics (he obviously didn't get the memo about avoiding the first three rows in Ms Green's classes, not without an umbrella, anyway), where he clearly doesn't engage with the wonders of the course outline any more than I do.

Ms Green is wearing what seems to be a peach-coloured dressing-gown. I can see dark leg-hairs squished between her skin and her beige pantyhose. She's surrounded by a cloud of hairspray that makes me wonder if she is a primary contributor to greenhouse gas emissions. Her blue eye shadow goes right up to her eyebrows, and then keeps going. As she lisps her way through the course outline, I consider the possibility that she might actually be a man.

New Guy stares dreamily off into space and doodles in the margins of the course outline. I snoop over his shoulder and see biro sketches of dragons, and knights with swords. What is this guy, *nine*? He is so going to get broken at this school. There's a strange, biscuity smell coming from him, which is not at all what I imagine boys should smell like.

As I'm watching, a little glistening glob of Ms Green's spit lands on his page, near the dragon. The New Guy pauses for a moment, and then draws around it, turning it into a crystal ball thingy being held by a wizard wearing a pointy hat. Oh. Dear.

I think he can feel me watching, because he turns and stares at me. His face isn't too bad – a little pudgy perhaps, with a blemish or two, but nothing that couldn't be fixed with a skin peel and a few weeks of no carbs after lunch. He has nice eyes.

He raises his eyebrows at me, and I blush and look away. Nice eyes notwithstanding, he's still obviously a Complete and Total Social Incompetent. I feel sorry for him, but not enough to actually, you know, *talk* to him or anything.

Not that my social status is so high or secure that me talking to the New Guy would automatically confer upon him some degree of coolness. I have, after many years of diligent eyebrow-waxing and lip-glossing, clawed my way out of the rotting mire of uncoolness, and am now desperately clinging to my own little rung of the social ladder. It's not a cool rung, but it's a normal rung, and that's good enough for me.

Tahni's way further up the ladder than me. I'm not quite sure how it happened, but at some point between Grade 6 and Year 9, she became cool. Her body shape-shifted to create pleasing curves, and her uniform suddenly clung and flared in all the right places as though it was personally tailored to make her look beautiful.

*My* uniform hangs off me like a shroud. I blame my mother. When we went to the uniform shop in Year 7, Mum decided that in order to save money and natural resources and to lessen the burden on the starving kids in China working in sweatshops, she would buy me the largest size there was, so I could 'grow into it'. I pointed out that the chances of me *tripling my body size* in six years was unlikely, and that when I did need a bigger uniform, it would be supplying more work to the starving sweatshop kids, but she just called me a capitalist and bought it anyway.

Four years on, the dress is (unsurprisingly) still enormous. Except now it has the added bonus of being rather threadbare from constant wearing and washing, and has a blue biro stain on the side from when my pen leaked in a Year 9 Geography test.

Lunch is much like recess, only worse. I waste time in the queue at the canteen (the boy in front of me orders a 'headjob' instead of a hedgehog and hilarity ensues), but before long I am once again subject to a long and painful interrogation by my best friend. I mumble and stutter through some outrageous lies about dates and kisses and gifts (he bought me a hardcover early edition of *The Secret Garden* — my favourite book). Tahni is like a vulture. It's quite scary.

'It's such a relief you finally have a boyfriend,' says Tahni. 'I worried about you.'

'Thanks,' I say. 'It's so nice to know you care.'

'Of course I care!' says Tahni, completely oblivious to my sarcasm. 'I was starting to think you might be—' she looks away and muffles a weird giggle.

'I might be what?' I say. 'Destined to end up a lonely old lady with eleven cats?'

'Never mind,' says Tahni.

I frown. 'No, what?' I don't like the idea that she thinks things about me without telling. *Oh poor Midge*, she probably thinks, *she's so boring and ugly that she'll never get a boyfriend. Not like me* (hair toss, re-apply lip gloss, hair toss).

'I thought—' says Tahni, then laughs again and examines her bare knees.

'You thought . . .'

'I thought you were a . . .' Tahni lowers her voice. 'A *thespian*.'

I raise my eyebrows. 'You thought I was an *actor*? After my shameful performance in the school production of *Ain't Misbehavin'* last year?'

'Not an actor,' says Tahni. 'I thought you might, you know. *Like girls.*'

I can't help laughing. 'You mean a *lesbian*, not a *thespian*.'

'Isn't it the same thing?' says Tahni.

I think I just figured out where all those curves came from. They migrated from her brain. And hang on a minute; she thought I was a *lesbian*? Just because I don't have a boyfriend? Not that there's anything *wrong* with being a lesbian. I'm just not one. Oh God, what if I am? What if that's why I've never had a boyfriend? I think about it for a minute. No. I don't think I am. I've listened to Dad's k.d. lang albums, and I feel nothing. And I like boys. The ones on television. I just haven't met any actual real boys that I like. Except for my imaginary boyfriend, of course.

'No,' I say. 'Not a lesbian. Or a thespian, for that matter. I just have very high standards.'

Tahni nods, understanding, even though she has lower standards than a burger joint's recruitment process. 'So when did you last hear from him?' she asks.

'He emailed me last night,' I say.

'Really?' says Tahni. 'And?'

'It's – ah . . . It's private,' I say. Brilliant answer. Brilliant. I am a genius. Of course it's private.

'Fail,' says Tahni. 'There's no such thing as privacy between friends. Remember when I first got my period and I made you check in case it was something else?'

I screw up my nose. 'How could I forget?'

'You need to tell me,' Tahni says. 'I can decipher the boy code.'

There's a *boy code*? Does all that monosyllabic grunting actually *mean* something? Is there a decoder ring for the 'your mum' jokes?

'Oh,' I say. 'I couldn't possibly do it justice. He has such a lovely turn of phrase, and I'm sure I would spoil it if I tried to remember.'

She nods.

Success!

'Well,' says Tahni. 'Print it. Bring it to school tomorrow.'

'Right,' I say. My voice sounds a bit squeaky.

'And Midge?'

I think I am going to be sick, but I smile at her.

'What's his name?'

Oh, crap.

## 3  scheme

/skim/

–noun; a plan, design, or program of action to be
followed; project.

– A Wordsmith's Dictionary of Hard-to-spell Words

B. His name needs to start with a B. B is for Beautiful and
Brave and Bold and Bright.

*Bert* means 'bright and glorious', but it makes me think
of *Sesame Street*, so that's no good. *Byron* is poetic but girly.
*Brian* is much more masculine and means strong, but I have
a weird cousin called Brian.

*Benjamin* means 'fortunate' or 'lucky'. And I will be both
lucky and fortunate if I can get myself out of this stupid
situation without looking like an idiot, so Benjamin it is.

*Dearest, loveliest Imogen,*

*I can't believe it's only been two weeks since I saw you last. It feels like
an age. I can't stop thinking about you. The photo I have, of us by the river,
is in danger of crumbling to dust; I am touching it so often. I wish it was
you that I was touching . . .*

Oh, dear. This isn't going well. Ben sounds like some kind of Mr Darcy-meets-pervert trench coat-wearing freak.

*Dear Imogen,*
  *I was reading Proust the other day, and I thought of you.*

Who is Proust, anyway? I google. Ooh, Marcel Proust wrote a book called *Remembrance of Things Past*. So Ben could be Remembering the Things that Passed when we spent time together. Very appropriate. And it's French. I'm sure Ben read it in the original French. Maybe in France, where his family has a little chateau that they visit in summer. I can just imagine him, sitting on an old wooden bench in a garden surrounded by green and pink and yellow flowers, and the light is all warm and lovely like a Van Gogh painting before he cut his ear off.

For about five seconds I consider learning French so I can go and hang out with Ben in the chateau and we could eat baguettes and read Proust to each other. But judging from his Wikipedia page, Proust's books are completely unintelligible even when they're in English, so I think I'll pass.

I read over the letter and think about adding a couple of spelling mistakes for authenticity. Maybe an *untill* or a *loose* instead of *lose*? But I just can't bring myself to do it. My boyfriend would know how to spell.

All of this lying has made me hungry. Why hasn't Mum called me for dinner yet? I open my bedroom door. No cooking smells. Odd. It's nearly seven-thirty.

Downstairs, Dad's sitting on the couch watching *Temptation*. Mum's so going to scorch him for watching commercial TV.

'Where's Mum?' I say.

Dad shrugs. 'Working late.'

He's engrossed by Livinia Nixon. I clear my throat.

'Was there something else?' says Dad.

'Yes,' I say. 'The troops are restless. The mess is closed.'

Dad looks up at me. 'What?'

'Dinner. It's seven-thirty. Feed me.'

'Oh,' says Dad, looking vague. 'Sorry. I had a late lunch. Do you want me to fix you some two-minute noodles?'

Two-minute noodles? Oh dear. I'll be in the cupboard under the stairs next, and I'll have to walk to school in the snow with no shoes or socks (we may have to move somewhere where it snows first), and then Family Services will come. And then they'll take me to an orphanage and some plucky freckled redhead will take me under her wing . . .

'There had better be chicken flavour,' I grumble. 'I'm not eating prawn again.'

I stay up half the night finishing Ben's letter. By the time I get to school the next morning, I look (and feel) like Steve Buscemi. Tahni hugs me sympathetically.

'You're pining,' she says.

She gushes over the letter and I feel quite proud. I'd even faked the whole email header thing with a To and From and Subject.

20

'He sounds perfect,' sighs Tahni. 'Romantic, but not *too* romantic.'

'That's what I was going for,' I say.

Oops. She raises her eyebrows.

'In a boyfriend,' I say, feeling my cheeks go pink. 'That's what I was looking for in a boyfriend. Romantic, but not too romantic.'

For a moment I think I'm going to get busted.

'It's good to have goals,' says Tahni.

Phew.


In English, Mr Mehmet tells us about our Big Assignment. We're supposed to do a project in pairs. I'm not really listening; I'm too busy trying to think of how to get out of this whole Ben mess. I can't break up with him yet — it's too soon. I need to string Tahni along for at least a fortnight. Then I can say that the whole long-distance thing is too much, and we decided to be just friends. But a whole fortnight? That's a lot of fake emails.

Someone is saying my name. I look up. Mr Mehmet is frowning down at me.

'When you've quite finished daydreaming, Imogen, perhaps you would like to choose a partner.'

I am *this close* to saying something about my boyfriend in England, but snap out of it and realise that everyone else has organised themselves into pairs. Everyone except for me. And the New Guy.

Oh, crap. I have to spend a whole lesson with Mr Socks Pulled Up Dragon Pictures. Bleck.

I collect my books, shuffle down to the front row and sit next to New Guy. He smiles and then ducks his head in a nervous kind of way. He still smells like biscuits.

'You and your partner must select a topic, and write a proposal by next week,' says Mr Mehmet.

Uh oh.

'You will then have the rest of the term to work on your project. Remember, it must contain an online component, as well as a written report, and a final analysis detailing how you came to your conclusion. You will present your projects to the entire year level at the end of term.'

This isn't just a one-off class project. I'm going to be lumped with New Guy for the rest of my life.

'All right,' says Mr Mehmet. 'You have the rest of the class to discuss your projects.'

New Guy turns to me. He has very long eyelashes. He also has a bit of white gunk in the corner of his left eye. Gross.

'Imogen, right?' he says. 'I'm George.'

'It's Midge,' I say. The biscuity smell is making me hungry.

I fiddle with my pen, popping the cap off and snapping it back on again. George straightens his exercise book against the edge of the table.

'So,' says George. 'What will we do for our project?'

I shrug. I'm quite busy enough with my imaginary-boyfriend project. I have no time to think about anything else.

'Dunno,' I say. 'Do you have any ideas?'

'It should be relevant to young people today,' he says. 'Something about the pressure placed on teenagers in modern society.'

This is all Ben's fault. If I hadn't been thinking about him I could have picked a better partner. Stupid imaginary boyfriend.


At lunchtime, I tell Tahni about being saddled with the New Guy.

'O.M.G.,' she says. 'You're doing your English project with *him*?'

I nod.

'But haven't you heard?'

'Heard what?'

Tahni leans in close. 'Why he left his old school. I'm not entirely sure what happened, but it was bad. Kate Martin says it was because he attacked another kid. They say the kid was in hospital for a month.'

I think about that for a moment. I think about New Guy, and his soft brown eyes and pulled-up socks.

'I doubt that,' I say.

'That's not all,' says Tahni. 'James O'Keefe told me that when he got suspended, they found all this stuff in his locker – all these pictures of swords and armour and stuff. Like he was planning something.'

I roll my eyes. 'Yeah, right,' I say. 'Underneath those long, dark lashes, New Guy has the cold hard instincts of a killer.'

The bell rings. Tahni grabs my arm and hisses dramatically into my ear.

'Just be careful,' she says. 'Remember Camembert.'

As I wander back to my locker, I rack my brains. Camembert? Was there an incident where someone was suffocated with soft cheese? Is she telling me to think of Ben, and our picnic with the squishy cheese and the daisy garland?

I'm half an hour into Maths before I realise she meant Columbine.

## 4 **er·satz**

/ˈɛrzæts/

–noun; an artificial substance or article used to
replace something natural or genuine;
a substitute.

– A Wordsmith's Dictionary of Hard-to-spell Words

I'm in my bedroom, staring at my computer. I should be writing my essay on the pros and cons of the Australian system of government, but instead I'm trying to figure out whether my imaginary boyfriend is a Facebook kind of imaginary boyfriend, or a MySpace kind of imaginary boyfriend.

I settle on MySpace, because it's more public. And more artsy. Ben is definitely artsy.

I wonder what kind of background my imaginary boyfriend would have on his MySpace page. Nothing too cheesy. Maybe a classy black-and-white photo of a lake or a tree or something. I do a half-hearted search on Google Images, but then decide against it. If he did have a photo, it would be one he took himself, with some kind of compelling story that went with it, like he saved a three-year-old child from drowning in that lake just seconds after he took the photo. And given Ben doesn't exist, it'll be pretty hard to find a photo he took.

Plain white is too simple. Ben pays a lot of attention to detail. I'll have to go with a solid colour. Black's too emo. I try a mossy green (too earth-mothery) and a classic brown (too Poncy English Tweed Tally-ho Old Chaps), before settling on a nice, muted blue.

Right. Interests.

**General:**    Photography, black-and-white movies, reading, <u>**lacrosse**</u>.

This is good. It shows he is the kind of boy who can talk about Hitchcock without sniggering, but is also athletic. Lacrosse is such a thinking-man's sport.

I think about adding 'writing poetry', but perhaps that's pushing it a bit. There is such a thing as Going Too Far.

**Music:**    <u>**This Broken Tree**</u>, <u>**The Beatles**</u>, <u>**Bob Dylan**</u>, <u>**Leonard Cohen**</u>

I don't really know much about music. I only know This Broken Tree because someone mentioned them in that TV show where ridiculously beautiful teenagers discover dead bodies in their swimming pools. All the others are from Dad's record collection. They seem like the kind of indie vintage music that Intellectual Boys might listen to.

The phone rings downstairs. I let Dad pick it up. It's probably Mum, who is working late again. More two-minute noodles for dinner. I'll have to talk to Dad about expanding our culinary repertoire, at least to include soup-in-a-can and maybe some instant mac-and-cheese.

**Movies:** **Rear Window**, **Psycho**, The Maltese Falcon, Gilda, **Finding Nemo**, The Muppets Take Manhattan.

I almost put *Casablanca* in, but even I've seen it, so I reckon it's too much of a cliché. *Finding Nemo* and *The Muppets Take Manhattan* are there so he doesn't look too much like a wanker.

'Midge!' Dad is knocking on my door. 'Phone for you.'

He opens the door with the cordless in his hand. I quickly minimise the MySpace project and tap away at my Politics essay.

'It's a *boy*,' says Dad, a delighted look on his face. Aren't Dads supposed to be all 'don't touch my daughter' protective? What happened to the Man-to-Man talk about how My Daughter is a Special and Precious Flower and If You Touch Her Breasts I'll Remove Your Kneecaps? Parents these days, I tell you.

I grab the phone off him, push him out the door and slam it shut, just as he starts singing that 'Ring Ring' song by Abba.

The stupid thing? I have no idea who might be on the phone. What boy? A boy has never called me. It's probably a telemarketer trying to sell me a dodgy phone plan. But the thing is, I have this funny, tickly, bubbly nervous feeling inside. Because even though it's not possible, I'm kinda hoping it's Ben, calling long-distance just to hear my voice.

I've never Talked To a Boy on the Phone before. What if I don't do it right? What if he loses interest because I don't know how to say the right things? What if he wants to . . . you know. Have *phone sex*? I am briefly consoled by the fact that Ben doesn't actually exist, but then the bubbles come up again because I really *want* it to be him.

Yeah, I'm crazy. I put the phone to my ear. 'Hello?'

It isn't Ben.

'Hi, it's George.'

For a moment, I think, *Who's George?* I don't know a George. Then I realise it's New Guy. Wizard-drawing, socks-pulled-up, biscuit-scented, long-eyelashes, Columbine-camembert New Guy.

'Oh,' I say, trying not to be too disappointed that my First Ever Phone Call From a Boy is not from my imaginary boyfriend, but instead from the daggy, possibly psychotic new kid who I have to do some lame project with in English. 'Hi.'

What if Tahni is right? What if he really is a killer? What if he's decided to fall in love with me and he's going to stalk me and take off my skin and then eat me alive?

'So I was thinking about our project,' he says.

'How did you get this number?' I interrupt. Maybe he's some sort of freakishly intelligent, evil hacker who's installed a miniature surveillance camera inside my toothbrush so he can watch me pee.

There is a slight pause. 'White Pages dot com,' he says. 'How else?'

I'm sure that's what all the serial killers say.

'So . . .' he says. 'The project?'

I wonder if Ben has seen *Silence of the Lambs*.

'I was thinking that we could do something about secrets,' he says.

I stiffen. What kind of secrets? His secret about the skinless women in his dungeon? Or does he know my secrets from watching via my toothbrush-cam? Does he know? He couldn't possibly.

'Secrets?' I say. My voice goes squeaky, and I cough to disguise it.

'You know,' he says. (I don't.) 'Like how even though we're living in an entirely connected world, where communication has never been so open and accessible, people still have just as many secrets as ever. If not more.'

I stare at Ben's MySpace page. New Guy doesn't know how right he is. At least I hope he doesn't know.

'Midge?' he says. 'Are you still there?'

I jerk back to the real world. 'Yep,' I say. 'Still here. Secrets. Fantastic.'

'So you think it's a good idea?'

'Sure,' I say. I hear it's a good idea to humour potential killers. 'But what would we actually do?'

'I don't know yet,' New Guy says. 'I did a bit of googling, and found a couple of quotes. Benjamin Franklin said, "Three can keep a secret, if two of them are dead."'

OMG. Did he just make a threat? Is he saying he's going to kill me? Who is Benjamin Franklin, anyway? Some dead American, I think.

'Ben clearly had a great deal of faith in humanity,' I say, stalling for time.

'Maybe he told someone something important, and they betrayed him.'

'Yeah,' I say, laughing nervously. 'Like that he's a closet *Star Trek* fan or something.'

Oh, don't tell me he likes *Star Trek* too. Could this guy be any more of a weirdo loser? A weirdo loser PSYCHO-KILLER?

But he chuckles. 'I would think,' he says, 'that if they had television in the eighteenth century, Benjamin Franklin's secret TV shame would be *Oprah*. Or the *Gilmore Girls*.'

I am not sure whether I should laugh. I don't want him to think I'm laughing *at* him. Don't want to upset the killer.

'So,' I say. 'Any more quotes?'

'One from Sophocles,' New Guy says. '"Do nothing secretly; for Time sees and hears all things, and discloses all."'

I'm confused now. All this double-speak. He says *Sophocles* with a bit of a strange accent, and I remember that Mrs Church called him *George Papadopoulos* and figure that he must be Greek.

'Sophocles also not a fan of the whole secret thing,' I observe.

'No,' says New Guy. 'Maybe that's what we should try to prove? Whether secrets are good or bad?'

I think about this. Secrets are harmless when they are about an imaginary English boyfriend, right? It's only bad when you've killed someone and hidden their body. 'Animals have secrets,' I say. 'Like where a nest or a den is, or where a dog has buried a bone.'

'Right,' says New Guy, who I suppose I should think of as George (or psycho-killer George). 'So there is a biological protective urge to keep secrets.'

I'm not entirely comfortable with Talking to a Boy on the Phone about Biological Urges. I wonder what Ben would say if he knew. Would he be jealous? What are you allowed to talk to Other Boys about when you're in a relationship? Where is the line between Having a Conversation with a Boy and Phone-Cheating? And where do Biological Urges lie in relation to that line?

'Let's brainstorm,' says (psycho-killer) George. 'Think of common secrets.'

Imaginary boyfriends. Psycho-killer. Imaginary boy-friends. Psycho-killer. Imaginary boyfriends.

'Surprise parties?' I manage to squeak out.

'Great,' he says. 'What about secrets that are to do with

not admitting something? Like: I broke the vase.'

'Or: I hate your new haircut.'

'Or: I ate the last Tim Tam.'

This is kind of fun. 'There's no Easter Bunny,' I say.

'I have a crush on someone,' says (psycho-killer) George, and I immediately feel uncomfortable again.

'Um,' I say. 'I think I'm all out of secrets.'

(Hah. That's a ginormous lie.)

(Psycho-killer) George is silent for a moment.

'What about big secrets?' he says. 'Like: I cheated on you.'

'I only have six months to live.'

'Your father is Darth Vader.'

I laugh. 'And that girl you just kissed is your sister!'

'I live a secret life,' says (psycho-killer) George.

A secret life as a murdering cannibal. I know your story.

'Like Superman and Clark Kent?' I ask.

'Maybe,' says (psycho-killer) George. 'But I meant something else . . . like I have another family or something.'

Yeah. Another family. Right. Maybe before he became a psycho-killer cannibal. Now his other family are chewed-up skeletons buried beneath the vegie patch.

'I prefer secret superpowers,' I say.

'Yeah, me too.'

I take a deep breath. 'How about the opposite?' I say. 'Instead of having a secret life or a secret superpower, a part of my life that seems real is actually fake.'

'Like what?'

Why am I saying this? Why am I practically confessing my terrible terrible shame to a murderer? 'I don't know,' I say. 'Like an imaginary friend or something. Pretending you have this great . . . job, when you're unemployed. Or pretending you're rich and live in a mansion when you're homeless.'

'Yeah . . .' says (psycho-killer) George, thoughtfully. 'Or that you have this perfect life with a perfect partner and perfect kids, when in fact you're all miserable.'

I swallow. 'Something like that,' I say.

This is very weird. I just came really close to telling the crazy psychotic serial killer socks-pulled-up New Guy that I have an imaginary boyfriend.

'You know what I think?' says George.

'What?'

'I think that Sophocles would have been totally addicted to *Big Brother*.'

## 5  chi·me·ra

/kɪˈmɪərə/

–noun; an unreal creature of the imagination; a vain
or idle fancy.

– A Wordsmith's Dictionary of Hard-to-spell Words

After a fortnight of fake emails and MySpace comments,
I am ready to break up with Ben. But I don't want to do it
straight away. It has to be believable. So I plant little seeds.
I sigh as Tahni and I eat our sandwiches at lunchtime. Ben
writes me long and tortured emails about how much
he misses me.

It's strange, because I'll miss him when we're broken up.
He's the perfect boyfriend – except for the whole Not Being
Real thing. That's a bummer. But still, I could certainly
do worse.

When I walk into school the next morning, Tahni is
waiting for me at my locker. Like a hungry shark. A hungry
shark who is about to explode with excitement. She
seriously looks like she's about to wet herself.

'Hey,' I say, fiddling with the combination lock on my
locker.

Tahni lets out an incoherent squeal, jumps up and down and flaps her hands. Is she having a seizure?

Maybe this is about the comment that Ben wrote on my MySpace last night: *Midge, I want to see you so much. It is so hard being apart.* It's step one in my plan for us to break up. A few more of them, and I'll be able to sigh and say that it Just Wasn't Working.

Tahni still hasn't managed to utter anything coherent.

'Calm down,' I tell her. 'Yoga breathing, remember? In through the nose, out through the mouth.'

She takes a deep breath.

'O.M.G.'

Maybe she met a new boy. Maybe she won the lottery. Maybe aliens took out her brain.

'Midge,' she says, gasping. 'I am so sorry. This is going to sound so bitchy, but when you first told me about Ben, I kinda maybe thought that you were making him up. Because no one else had seen him, and you've never even *looked* at a boy before.'

I nod and smile.

'And I just wanted to apologise,' Tahni continues. 'For not trusting you.'

Ahh, the marvels of the internet. I put my books away, stacking them in alphabetical order. Last year I ordered them by colour, which looked very pretty but was ultimately confusing.

'So have you spoken to him yet, this morning?'

'No,' I say, laughing. 'It's the middle of the night in England.'

Tahni gives me a playful slap. 'You don't need to keep going on with this game,' she says. 'I know your secret.'

Oh, crap. How did she figure it out? Was it the MySpace page? Was the blue background not masculine enough?

'Why didn't you tell me?' she says.

'Um,' I say, ready to confess.

'I can't believe you didn't tell me Ben was definitely moving to Australia *and* coming to our school!'

Huh?

'Come on,' she says, grabbing my arm. 'Chris Stitz told me where his locker is. I'm *dying* for an introduction.'

I think I'm having a stroke. I wonder if I've slipped into a parallel universe. Or if this is a terrible cruel joke and there's a film crew on standby, ready to catch my moment of ultimate humiliation. Why would Tahni say that Ben was here? Maybe she's just teasing me. Maybe my imagination is so powerful that he turned into a Real Boy, like Pinocchio.

Everything goes all fuzzy, and it's like time speeds up, because I can't get a word out before suddenly I'm standing in front of this Boy.

He's tall, with lovely light-brown wavy hair that is exactly the right length. He has good skin (v. important), and is toned without being muscly. He has *heavenly* shoulders. His eyes are exactly the same colour blue as the background on his MySpace page. He's not exactly the way I pictured

Ben in my head, but he still looks pretty good.

I think Tahni was expecting someone a bit less . . . well, *hot*. I'd described him as a cute nerd, but this guy is just plain hot. When she sees him, it's like watching a double take from an old Warner Brothers cartoon. Her chin hits the ground. *Smack.* But in true Tahni fashion, she pulls herself together and summons her most dazzling smile.

'Hi Ben,' she says. 'I brought you a surprise!'

She shoves me forward. The Boy looks at me, as if I'm a Transformer and he's expecting me to turn into a Mac truck or something.

'We were *so* excited when we found out Midge's boyfriend was moving here!' Tahni rabbits on, not noticing the Boy's confusion. 'She's told us all about how you met over summer. *So* romantic!'

The Boy keeps looking at me, like he's waiting for something. An explanation, probably. I want to dissolve into a puddle. This has *got* to be a dream. There is a terrible, terrible silence. I stare at my shoes, waiting for the inevitable. My cheeks are burning and I'm afraid I might burst into tears. That would just totally be the final nail in the already hermetically sealed coffin that is my life.

Tahni is still babbling. 'I admit I thought Midge would never get a boyfriend. I thought she'd end up cutting off her hair and wearing polar fleece and kissing girls, or that she'd just be lonely and old with eleven cats and a caravan.'

Thanks, Tahni, for all your wonderful support.

'When she told me she'd met this boy called Ben over summer and how he was English and sensitive, I thought she must be making it up. You sounded too good to be true.'

A flicker of understanding passes over the Boy's face. He's figured it out. My terrible secret shame.

'Well?' says Tahni. 'Aren't you going to kiss her hello?'

Please let this be a dream. I silently beg this Boy to put me out of my misery quickly. He still has a slightly puzzled frown on his face, and a strange little half-smile. The moment drags on forever. If time sped up before, it's completely stopped now. It's as if we stand there for hours, Tahni expectant, the Boy confused, and me, slowly melting into something wet and sticky, like Gatorade, but without the electrolytes. I am radioactive. No one will ever speak to me again. I'll have to change schools. Change my name. Maybe go on *Extreme Makeover*, get a new face and a new identity and start again. Only then will I be able to escape this terrible, terrible shame.

The Boy opens his mouth to say something, then shuts it again. I plead with my eyes. My eyes tell him everything that's happened and about how sorry I am and how I will never do it again, not that I will have the chance to because I will never again have friends to lie to, and can he please get this over with because I need to go home and see if there's enough money in my piggy-bank to get plastic surgery.

I wonder what you have to do to qualify for a witness protection program?

Suddenly, the Boy speaks. To me. He speaks to me. He really *is* English, with this lovely soft accent that makes him sound like he's the star of one of those English Provincial Cop Shows set in a green and floral Quaint English Village where everyone calls each other 'guvnor' and there is a disproportionately high rate of crime.

'Sugar,' he says. 'I missed you so much.'

And then he steps forward and kisses me.

## 6 **cock·a·ma·mie**

/ˈkɒkəˌmeɪmi/

–adjective; ridiculous, pointless, or nonsensical.

– A Wordsmith's Dictionary of Hard-to-spell Words

I am kissing a Boy. I am being kissed by a Boy.

A real boy. A not-imaginary Boy.

It's a little more . . . moist . . . than I expected. And I know I'm meant to stick my tongue in, but then what do I do with it? Magazines should be more specific. Also, our teeth bump a couple of times, and that's Not Good.

My hands are on his shoulders – Ben's heavenly shoulders – they feel as strong as they look. His hands are on my waist. I am up on tiptoes to reach him, and I'm going to develop a serious crick in my neck if this continues for much longer. Not to mention running out of oxygen and asphyxiating.

But who cares about breathing and neck-cricks and tongues and teeth and moistness?

I. Am. Kissing. A. Real. Live. Boy.

A small part of me wonders what everyone else in the hallway is doing. In my head, it unfolds like this:

*Ben and I are kissing. There is space all around us, because people are so in awe of our love that they dare not approach us. But they are watching from the sidelines. Tahni is open-mouthed with astonishment and a hint of jealousy. Hundreds of students and teachers stop what they are doing and watch. Their eyes mist over with emotion, and silly smiles spread across their faces. The camera pans around us and upwards in a spiral that reveals the enormity of our love. Music swells.*

Am I wearing the pair of school tights with the hole that Mum never fixed? I think I am. All of those people, staring at the hole in my tights. And I should have polished my shoes. And they can all see the ink stain on my school dress. Did I brush my hair this morning?

*Did I brush my teeth!????*

I break away from the Boy, who does this adorable little sardonic eyebrow raise at me. I look around. Nobody is paying any attention at all, apart from Tahni, who is open-mouthed, exactly as I imagined.

And that's when it hits me.

I have magic superpowers. I invent a hot English imaginary boyfriend, and here he is, with his right hand still on my waist. Whatever I say comes true! I am King Midas, but with truth instead of gold. I speak and it happens. Mr Mehmet – get me another partner for the English project! It's time to buy a lottery ticket.

What else could it be? A coincidence? Pretty wild coincidence. And if it is, then why is Ben playing along? What's in it for him? *Surely* it's more than that. You don't kiss someone like that just because you're playing along. I have a micro-flashback to the kissing, and my knees feel weak.

The bell rings for form assembly. Ben takes his hand off my waist and turns to his locker. I feel like I've had a body part removed. Put that hand back, Mister. He pulls books out of his locker.

My lips are tingling as though they've been sprinkled with fairy dust or washing powder or something. I want more. I've become a kissing-obsessed maniac in all of five minutes. How long till recess?

I take another good look at Ben. He is gorgeous. He makes the school uniform stylish and debonair. He's just the right height. We'll look so good together. We'll parade the school grounds every recess and lunch, holding hands. People will sigh with jealousy. I wonder what he'll wear to our wedding. We'll have a holiday house by the sea and our beautiful children will play in the sand and we'll sit up on the deck wearing cable-knit jumpers and drinking wine. We'll be photographed for a home decorating magazine.

Tahni is leaning forward, staring Ben's books as if they're going to explain this unlikely turn of events.

Hah! Who's got the amazing boyfriend now, eh Tahni? No more teasing about V-plates, no more jokes about being old and crocheting little coats for my seven hundred cats.

There is clearly such a thing as karma, because while I'm thinking these uncharitable thoughts, Tahni frowns.

'I thought Midge said your surname was Hopkins?' she points at Ben's diary, which has *Benjamin L Wheeler* written on it in black Sharpie.

The game is up. The party is over. The fat lady has handed in her invoice and called a taxi. At least I got to kiss a boy once before I died of shame. Ben does the cute eyebrow thing again. And he *winks*.

'My parents just broke up,' he says, smooth as butter. 'I'm using my mum's name now. That's why we moved here.'

'Oh,' says Tahni. 'I'm sorry.'

Ben shrugs. 'It's no big deal.'

Definitely superpowers. The corridor is almost empty now, everyone's gone to class.

'So what does the *L* stand for?' asks Tahni. 'Midge said your middle name was Oliver.'

Come on, Ben. Help me out here.

'Um,' he says, shrugging.

No. Not after we've come so far.

'He has two middle names,' I say quickly. 'Oliver and . . .'

'Luke,' says Ben.

'Luke!' I repeat. 'Luke and Oliver. His two middle names.'

Tahni glances from Ben to me suspiciously. I hold my breath for approximately seven squillion years. Then Tahni and I speak at the same time.

She says, 'So why don't you—'

Just as I yell out, 'BLOW!'

Tahni and Ben both look surprised.

'When he changed his surname, it meant that his initials were B. L. O. W. *Blow*. Which isn't good, is it?'

They both shake their heads. Thank you, Grade 6 spelling bee. Thank you.

'And,' I say, now on a spelling-roll. 'If he'd used Oliver, then it would have been B.O.W. Which would have been *Bow*. Like *bow-wow*, a dog. That's why he started using his other middle name.'

I blush. Ben raises his eyebrows.

'You just remember everything, don't you, sugar?' he says.

Tahni is disappointed. It's like she doesn't want me to have a boyfriend.

'I'll see you at recess,' I say. It's a brush-off, and a mean one, but she needs to stop interrogating Ben.

'Right,' she says. She has a funny expression on her face. 'Nice to meet you, Ben.'

'Likewise,' he says as she walks off.

And then I am alone. Alone with my No Longer Imaginary Entirely Perfect Boyfriend. What do I do now?

'We should talk,' he says.

I nod, suddenly feeling the wave of shame again. I can feel my face growing blotchy and red. He stares at me, waiting. The half-smile is still there. He's so gorgeous. I wonder what would happen if I just started kissing him again. Maybe I could just kiss him forever, and we'd never have to have this conversation.

'Well?' he says.

'Um,' I say, my voice hoarse. 'Maybe we can talk at recess.'

If I can ever escape Tahni's clutches.

Ben looks at me like I've just suggested we join an acrobatic troupe.

'Recess?' he says.

'Yeah,' I reply. 'It's at eleven, after third period.'

He raises his eyebrows. 'Why wait till recess?'

I laugh nervously. 'Because we have form assembly now? Then classes? The teachers get kinda antsy when there are no kids in the classes. It's part of the student/teacher symbiotic dynamic.'

'Whatever,' he says. 'Let's go.'

I've never wagged school before. I know that sounds insane, but I just haven't. I *like* school. Even the boring classes. I figure it's all stuff I'll need to know one day. Except for those stupid 'practical' Maths problems that ask things like, 'You are travelling north at 25 kph in a blue car. You have a chicken. How many eggs will the chicken have laid by the time you reach the red car?' Practical in the sense of *not at all*.

While I'm doing this mental babble routine, Ben turns and walks down the corridor. It's a really nice walk. Smooth and graceful and strong. I weigh up my choices.

If I stay, he'll think I'm a square. And then he might not like me any more and he'll tell everyone my secret and I may as well just quit school and learn how to crochet.

If I go, I might get caught. I might miss out on some Important Learning. But I also might get to do some more kissing.

I follow him. I wonder where we'll go. The library? A broom cupboard? A boiler room? (Does this school have a broom cupboard or a boiler room? Or are they just rooms for TV schools so kids can go and have secret trysts and get attacked by vampires?) Hide down behind the bike sheds? Where do all the other kids go to wag? Is there some secret bunker where they hang out, smoking rollie cigarettes and playing poker?

He's almost at the front door of the school.

'Wait!' I say. 'Where are you going?'

Ben shrugs. 'Out.'

I think I am having a heart attack. 'That's the front door,' I explain. 'Someone'll see. If you want to leave, you should at least sneak out the back way or something. There're some bushes that cover the back fence near the portables. If you give me a boost I can climb over. Unless Mrs Peck is doing fitness testing in P.E. – then there'll be kids on the oval and they'll be able to see us. Maybe we could change into P.E. uniforms and pretend to be running laps, but then swerve off when she's not looking, and duck behind the toilet block.'

Ben turns and saunters back to me. He stands very close. I thought boys were supposed to smell bad? Ben smells very, very good. 'You're funny,' he says, brushing a piece of hair away from my face. 'I like that.'

He likes me. He touched me. I feel like jelly — wobbly and transparent. He takes my hand (*my hand! We're holding hands!*) and leads me out the front door.

The whole time, I'm expecting sirens to sound, and attack-dogs to spring from nowhere, and creepy black vans with no windows to screech to a halt outside Reception as bulletproof-vested commandos drop from the trees. We're going to get caught. I'll be expelled. I'll have to beg for a job in the chicken and chip shop on High Street and I'll have six kids all to different fathers by the time I'm nineteen and there'll be photos of me in all the trashy magazines, falling out of taxis with no knickers on. *Such a shame*, everyone'll say. *She had so much promise, what with the Spelling Bee and all. What happened?*

I don't say any of this to Ben, of course. There's a fine line between 'You're funny, I like that' and 'Get away from me you crazed lunatic freak', and I'd like to stay on the side of that line that includes hand-holding and kissing.

We don't get caught. We waltz out the front door and down the steps, and right out the gate onto the street. Bold as brass. And nobody even notices.

If I'd known it was this easy, I might have done it before.

We go to a cafe ('Little Coffee in the Big Wood's'), and I order hot chocolate and immediately feel like a child when Ben asks for a long black. He's so sophisticated. I pay, in the hope that caffeine-related-bribery will make me seem like a mature, confidant lady-pays kind of girl.

We sit at a black laminex table. I fiddle with the sugar sachets and wonder if I should tell the waitress about the errant apostrophe in 'Wood's'.

'So,' he says.

'So,' I reply. I suddenly feel sick. This is embarrassing. He's hot and sophisticated and I can't stop looking at his lips.

'How did you know I was moving to your school?' he asks.

'I didn't,' I answer. 'How could I? We've never met. I just—'

And then it all pours out. I tell him about how I've never had a boyfriend, and how Tahni teases me, and how I made up Ben from England, and then there he was. He listens, nodding and doing his gorgeous little eyebrow thing. I can't tell what he's thinking, but he's not laughing at me, which is a start. He also hasn't run away screaming, or called an ambulance to escort me to a mental hospital.

'So this is all some kind of weird coincidence,' he says at last.

I nod. 'Thanks for covering for me.'

Our drinks arrive and he stirs sugar into his coffee. Maybe he really does like me. Maybe he understands. Maybe he's never had a girlfriend. Although I'm sure no one could be such a good kisser without putting in some serious practice hours. Maybe he'll find my eccentric imagination endearing. Maybe he'll fall in love with my mind.

'So you made me a MySpace page?' he says with a grin.

'Yep.'

'This was a pretty elaborate scheme of yours,' he says.

'If you're going to do something, may as well do it properly.'

'Can I have the address?' he asks. 'I might have a few suggestions.'

I write the address on a napkin for him. He picks up the napkin, then puts it down and slides it back across the table.

'You'd better put your phone number on there, too,' he says.

!!!!!!!!!!!!!!!!!!

## 7  al·i·ment

/'æləmənt/

–noun; 1.  that which nourishes; nutriment; food.
2.  that which sustains; means of support.

– A Wordsmith's Dictionary of Hard-to-spell Words

I can smell it from the driveway. My mouth waters. The smells get stronger and stronger as I open the door and slip into the hallway.

Food. Real food. Garlic and onions and meaty smells.

Mum's home.

I walk into the kitchen and stop, shocked.

It's like Martha Stewart exploded in here.

There are bowls of sugar and whisked eggwhites and cut-up strawberries and actual real fresh vegetables and pots and pans and delicious, sizzling sounds. Mum is standing in the middle of it all, wearing an apron, her hands dusted with flour.

'Hi, darling,' she says.

I stare at her and all the food, swooning a little at the wonderful smells. 'Is this some kind of *Funniest Home Kitchens* reality show?'

She laughs. 'What are you talking about?'

I wave a hand to take in the craziness of our kitchen. 'When did our house turn into the set for a cooking show?' I narrow my eyes. 'Is Jamie Oliver hiding in one of our cupboards?'

Mum stirs something smooth and brown and gravy-like on the stove with one hand, and opens the oven with the other and peers inside.

'Wait,' I say. 'Stop the presses. You're cooking a *roast*?'

Mum looks at me. 'Yes, I am' she says. 'What's the big deal?'

*What's the big deal?* She asks. The big deal? The last roast Mum made was a tofu and nutmeat loaf. (Yes, it was revolting. Yes, Dad and I snuck out to McDonalds afterwards. Yes, there are still leftovers in the freezer.). Mum hates cooking meat, especially red meat. Especially a big hunk of meat that was once a cow. Now she's stirring something pale and creamy that looks like cake mix.

'You're making a cake as well?' I ask.

'Lord, no,' she says, and I sigh with relief. It is my mother after all, not some creepy culinary cyborg.

'No,' she continues, still stirring. 'This is for Yorkshire puddings to serve with the beef. We're having pavlova for dessert.'

I am actually speechless. My mouth hangs open. This is not my mother. This is someone else's mother. This is the kind of mother who makes sandwiches with normal fillings, like peanut butter or cheese and vegemite. The kind of mother who slices carrots into sticks and bakes muffins and buys white bread. Not the kind of mother who makes her poor only child eat tahini and home-grown sprout sandwiches on wheat-free soy and linseed bread on her very first day at school.

Mum starts spooning the Yorkshire pudding batter into an oily muffin tray.

'Mum,' I finally manage. 'Someone died, didn't they? And you want to break it to me gently. Just tell me, okay?'

Mum shakes her head, smiling. 'Don't be ridiculous, Imogen,' she says. 'I thought it would be nice to have a family dinner. I've been working a lot recently, and I wanted to make it up to you and your father by cooking something special.'

She passes me a basket of fresh crusty bread rolls.

'Put these on the table, will you?'


The phone rings during dinner. I remember Ben has my phone number, and I hastily swallow my mouthful of roast potato in case it's him. What if it is? What will I say? I'll have to be witty. He likes it when I'm funny. But not too witty, because I don't want to seem like I'm trying too hard. My hands tremble.

Dad answers the phone.

'Hello?' he says, and then listens, his eyes flicking to me. 'Yes, but she's having dinner at the moment. She'll call you back when she's finished.' He pauses, listening again, and then gropes for a pen. 'Uh-huh,' he says. 'Okay. Bye.'

He hangs up, sits down again, and helps himself to another serve of beans. My fists are clenched so tight that I have little half-moon dints in my palms where my fingernails have dug in.

'Who was it?' I ask, trying to sound casual.

Dad winks at me. 'Another *boy*,' he says, and then shakes his head, grinning. 'You're growing up so fast.'

Oh. Oh. 'Was it the same boy as the other night?' I ask. 'Or a different boy?'

Dad shrugs. 'It's so hard to keep track,' he says.

'Wait,' says Mum. 'Do you have a *boyfriend*, Imogen?'

I feel myself go red. 'No,' I say, as I have a particularly vivid flashback to The Kiss this morning.

Mum and Dad share this meaningful *Oh, we're so proud our daughter is growing up to be a functioning heterosexual member of the adult species, and she won't spend the rest of her life crocheting little hats for seven million cats* look.

I stare at my plate for a moment, but I have to know.

'So who was it, Dad?' I ask.

'Who do you want it to be?' Dad replies. 'Do you have a *crush*?'

He and Mum titter. I'm about ready to throw the gravy boat at Dad's head, but before I have the chance, the phone rings again. Dad raises his eyebrows.

'Hello?' says Dad. 'Yes, she's here . . . No . . . She'll have to call you back later . . . Okay . . .' He scribbles on the notepad again. 'Okay. Bye.'

'*Another* boy?' asks Mum, as Dad sits back down in

slow motion, looking ready to spring into action if the phone rings again.

Dad grins. 'They'll be breaking down the door soon.'

'Gosh,' says Mum.

'Who was that?' I ask, trying not to clench my teeth.

'Prince William,' says Dad. 'He has a glass slipper he wants you to try on.'

I shove an entire potato into my mouth. 'Okay,' I say, chewing furiously. 'I've finished. Thanks for dinner, Mum, it was lovely. I've got a ton of homework.'

I leave the room, deftly swiping the message pad from the phone-table.

As I walk up the stairs to my room I glance at it.

*George 9078 1423*
*Ben 9093 7288*

He called! Ben called me! I should call him back. No. Wait. I need a plan.

I sit cross-legged on my bed and strategise. Charming, but not sycophantic. Funny, but not weird. Available, but not desperate.

I'm going to bring all the roast back up. I'm trembling and sweating and there is something inside me jumping around. I never really understood that phrase *butterflies in my stomach*. Now I do, except instead of butterflies, I have elephants wearing butterfly costumes bouncing about with the Yorkshire puddings and roast potato.

I do yoga-breathing. I am the essence of calm. My chakras are resonating on the frequency where serenity resides. I am in control.

I glide, serene and peaceful as a swan, outside to the landing and grab the cordless extension. Clutching the message pad page in one sweaty hand, I press the 'talk' button, only to hear my mother's voice in the receiver. Crap, she's on the phone.

'I can't, Jason,' she says. 'Not tonight.'

They seriously want her to go into work now? It's eight-thirty! There is no way I'm ever becoming a lawyer.

'Alice, please—' says a male voice, but my mum cuts him off.

'No, Jason. I need to spend time with my family.' She hangs up.

Hah! Take that, Jason. Evil lawyer scumbag. He probably wanted her help throwing poor people out of their houses. Or kicking orphans in the shins. Or knocking down little old ladies when they're crossing the road.

I am inspired by Mum's firm attitude. I dial Ben's number, and he answers on the third ring. My calmness dissolves like Aspro Clear – leaving a bubbly, fizzy feeling instead.

'Hi,' I say. My voice sounds like I'm being strangled. 'It's Midge.'

'Hi,' he says. I love his English accent.

I wonder what his bedroom's like. I know he must live around here somewhere, but I picture him in a charming whitewashed English cottage, surrounded by rambling trails of ivy and hedgehogs and men with pipes and waistcoats.

'So I've been checking out my MySpace page,' he says. 'And I've got a couple of changes I need you to make.'

'Um, okay,' I say. This is weird.

'I hate the Beatles,' he says. 'And I have absolutely no idea who Leonard Cohen is.'

'Yeah,' I say, laughing. 'Me either.'

Although I do quite like that *Hallelujah* song he sings.

'Okay,' I say again. I sit down at my desk and log on to MySpace. 'So what music do you like?'

Actually, this could be fantastic! I can find out all his interests. If I know what he likes, then I'll know what to say to make sure he likes me!

'I don't know,' Ben says. His voice is warm and quiet and intimate. 'Top 40 stuff, I suppose. Whatever's on the radio.'

Hmm. Not very helpful.

'On to movies,' he says. 'Black-and-white movies are boring – change it to the new James Bond, and *Spiderman*. And seriously, Midge, *Muppets Take Manhattan*? What am I, *five*?'

'It's cult,' I say. I like the Muppets.

'Whatever,' he says.

We update the rest of his profile.

'Um,' I say. 'I can give you the login details so you can do this yourself.'

'Nah,' he says. 'I'd rather you did it.'

I smile as I understand what's going on. This whole conversation is just an excuse for him to talk to me! He wants me to find out all about him. It's very cute, really. I'm glad I'm not the only one who finds this whole getting-to-know-each-other thing a little nerve-wracking.

We talk for one whole hour. He tells me about his old school in England, and about his English friends. It sounds like he misses them a lot. It must be hard moving to a new country, having to make new friends and start at a new school. I ask him if the schoolwork is very different.

'Don't know yet,' he says. 'I'll let you know when I finally make it to a class.'

So he didn't go back to school after we had coffee this morning. He must be finding it difficult to settle in.

I bite my lip. I am the only friend he has at school. He *needs* me!

He'll rely on me to show him where the library is, and tell him who he should hang out with and who pashed who at the social last year and how he should never eat the chicken-in-a-roll from the canteen if he wants to live to see his twenties.

This entertains me for a moment, until . . .

O.M.G.

That's why he likes me! Because he doesn't know anyone else at school. Once he meets the cool kids, and figures out my place on the social ladder, that's it. I'm gone. He'll swan off in a haze of popularity, and I'll be left behind, alone and heartbroken.

'I'd better go,' Ben says, interrupting my mental panic. 'I have stuff to do.'

'Okay,' I say. This is it – the beginning of the end.

'Bye, then.'

'Ben,' I say, desperate to keep him on the phone. It may be the last time.

'Mm?'

'Thanks. For understanding about the whole imaginary boyfriend thing. For not telling anyone.'

He chuckles. 'I'm sure I'll figure out a way for you to make it up to me.'

Is he talking about more kissing?

'See you tomorrow, Midge,' he says, and hangs up.

I hold the phone to my ear, listening to the dial tone and remembering the tickly, whispering feeling of his voice. I think I might have died and gone to heaven. Is this what it feels like to be in love?

*See you tomorrow.* He wants to see me. He likes me.

He likes me!

## 8  ex·ul·ta·tion

/ˌɛgzʌl'teɪʃən/

–noun; the act of exulting; lively or triumphant joy,
as over success or victory.

– A Wordsmith's Dictionary of Hard-to-spell Words

I am on fire. I am glowing so much I can't believe everyone isn't wearing sunglasses. People should be paying money to sit next to me, instead of going to the solarium.

Ben and I have been going out for three weeks. Everything is perfect. Kids who never even noticed me before are saying 'Hi' in the corridors. Having a boyfriend is an instant ticket to being popular. Particularly when the boyfriend in question is gorgeous and has such excellent shoulders.

I go straight to Ben's locker. He smiles, then grabs my wrist, pulls me towards him and kisses me.

And I die and float up to heaven. Again, I hope people see. I hope they all feel jealous.

'See you at recess,' he says, when he finally pulls away.

'. . .'

I am breathless and dizzy and can't manage more than a monosyllabic squeak.

Ben winks at me and saunters away. I hope he actually goes to class today.

In English, Mr Mehmet rambles on about Narrative Voice in *The Go-Between*, and I glow. I feel like I'm the centre of the universe. Everyone is gazing at me in awe, marvelling at my beauty and the adoration of the wondrous, wondrous boy who enjoys putting his face against mine and exchanging saliva.

'Okay,' says Mr Mehmet, after what I'm sure was a thousand years of droning, but feels like three seconds to me. Time must move differently when you're the centre of the universe. 'You can spend the rest of the class working on your projects with your partners.'

I float away on my cloud of happiness, until George slides into the seat next to me. He's dimming my glow. I wish he'd just disappear. How come I had to get *this* New Guy for my project?? Why can't I do mine with Ben? What if George chops me up into little pieces? Ben will die of grief and it will be totally *Romeo and Juliet*.

George pulls out the proposal we wrote for Mr Mehmet last week. Mr Mehmet thought it was a fantastic idea. Unfortunately we still haven't figured out what our online component will be. I sneak a peek at his folder and am silently impressed that he spelled 'acknowledgements' correctly. It's a toughie.

'Maybe we should look at the way secrets interact with technology,' says George.

'Maybe,' I say, thinking it sounds complicated. 'Like how

we used to write stuff in real-life diaries with locks and keys, and now we do it on a blog or a MySpace page where anyone can see it.'

'Yeah,' says George. Then he laughs.

'What?' I say.

'Never mind,' says George, still smiling.

'No,' I say. 'Tell me.'

'When I was little, my sister gave me her old Care Bears toy. It was called Secret Bear.'

I laugh. 'You had a *Care Bear*?' I say. 'That's not very masculine.'

'It was a hand-me-down,' he says defensively. 'I had lots of Lego as well.'

'Uh-huh.'

'Anyway,' says George. 'It had this cord in its back. And when you pulled it, it said things like *I'm Secret Bear* and *Do you have a secret?* and *I promise I won't tell.*'

George says all these things in a hammy American accent.

'Technology,' I say. 'Secrets. I'm with you.'

He nods. 'I used to tell all my secrets to Secret Bear,' he says. 'And then one day I was playing with him in the garden, when my sister said that if I told him too many secrets, he might get sick and explode with them all.'

I raise my eyebrows. 'This is why I'm glad I'm an only child,' I say.

'I was really upset,' says George. 'I ran inside, leaving Secret Bear in the garden. It rained that night.'

'Oh dear,' I say.

'The next morning, he was all wet, and there was a slug on his nose. I told him I was sorry, and then pulled his cord to see if he'd forgiven me.'

'And?'

'And he sounded like this,' George clears his throat, and talks in a slow, gravelly voice like a zombie. 'I-I-I'm See-ee-ee-cret Be-heh-heh-ear.'

I burst out laughing. Mr Mehmet glares at me.

'And I thought he was sick because I'd told him too many secrets.'

'So what did you do?' I ask.

George shrugs. 'I put him in a box and never told him a secret again.'

'That's a very sad story, George,' I say, still laughing.

'I really missed having someone to tell my secrets to,' he said. 'Someone who I knew would keep them no matter what . . .'

He frowns, as if he's just thought of something. His forehead goes all wavy and his long eyelashes quiver.

'What is it?' I ask.

'I think I'm having an idea,' says George.

'Don't strain yourself,' I reply.

'Do you know about PostSecret?'

I don't.

'It started as a project this guy did where he left blank postcards in public places, addressed to himself, and a note encouraging people to write down a secret and post it back.'

'What kind of secrets?'

'Everything. People wrote about how they were cheating on their wives, or that they ran over their neighbour's cat, or that they liked the smell of their own farts.'

'Gross,' I say.

'He got heaps of responses. But the amazing thing was, when the blank postcards ran out, people kept sending him secrets. They still do. Thousands and thousands of them. He's got a website.'

'What does he do with the secrets?' I ask.

George shrugs. 'Publishes the good ones,' he says. 'And keeps the others.'

'So what's the point?'

'It gives people a chance to reveal things they're scared to admit. Without fear of judgement, because it's all anonymous.'

'But they're not really telling anyone. It's not like they know him.'

'That's not the point. Just the act of writing it down and posting it makes people feel better.'

Sounds a bit strange to me.

'So what's your idea?' I ask.

'We do it. We set up a website where students can upload pictures or draw or write about their secrets.'

Actually, that's not bad.

'We can analyse them to see what issues are concerning teenagers,' I say. 'Like dressing the right way, and being thin, and being popular.'

George nods. 'And we can send an email to everyone in the school telling them about it. We can also have a page where you can read other people's secrets. It's visual, dynamic, interactive and fun.'

I smile. 'George, it's a fantastic idea.'

He actually blushes. 'So, do you want to get together after school and work on it?'

At this point, I'm reasonably sure that George isn't a serial killer. But there's no point taking chances.

'Um,' I say. 'I think I have something on.'

George looks awkward. He can probably tell I'm lying. 'Oh,' he says. 'What sort of something?'

'I'm not sure,' I say. 'I left my diary at home. But I remember I had something I had to do.'

'Well, do you want me to come by your house this evening after you've done it?'

I once saw a movie about how you should never invite a serial killer into your home. Or was that vampires?

'We're having our floors re-sanded,' I improvise. 'It's really gross at my house.'

George raises his eyebrows. Then he tears a sheet of paper out of an exercise book and scribbles something on it.

'This is my address and phone number,' he says. 'I'll be home all evening if you want to do some work.'

Very funny. As if I'm going to the house of a serial killer. I'm not stupid.

At recess, I can't find Ben anywhere. So I go and sit with

Tahni. I tell her about talking to Ben on the phone and how he kissed me this morning. Tahni's a bit quiet. She's probably jealous because all of a sudden I'm the one with the Boy-stories. Either that or she's got her period. Actually, she's been strange all week. Maybe she's mad because I was supposed to call her last night, but I called Ben instead.

I'm telling her about the way Ben's mouth curls in that little half-smile right before he kisses me, when I catch sight of the man himself. And he's headed straight for me.

I quickly fluff my hair, and debate whether to apply lip gloss. If I do, I'll look cuter, and he's more likely to want to kiss me again. But if I do end up kissing him, I don't want to get him all smeared with Juicy Berry. While I'm still mentally debating this (who thought boys and dating and kissing would be so hard!?), it all becomes irrelevant because he sits next to me, draping his arm around me. I can feel his leg pressed up against my leg. He nods at Tahni.

'Morning ladies,' he says, then nuzzles my neck.

I am in love. Any doubt I had about this has gone.

Imaginary Ben can just rack off. Imaginary Ben would never have *nuzzled* my neck like this. Imaginary Ben might have written me a poem, which would have been nice. But it wouldn't make me feel like I feel now.

An entire symphony orchestra explodes inside me in a sparkling shower of fireworks.

'Hi, Ben,' says Tahni, turning her most dazzling smile onto him.

'Hey,' he says, pulling away from my neck. I feel like I've lost a body part.

I'm not really sure how she does it, but in an instant Tahni manages to transform from sullen and bored to bright-eyed and gloss-lipped. She's shifted position slightly to accentuate her curvy hips and breasts, while still managing to show off her tiny, tiny waist. I frown. Is she *flirting* with my boyfriend?

'So are you settling in?' she asks him, fiddling with her hair.

'Yeah,' says Ben. His hand slides around my waist. Hah. Take that, Tahni.

'How are you going with your IT assignment?' Tahni asks.

They have a *subject* together? That's so unfair. I don't have any classes with Ben. Or with Tahni, for that matter. Just with stupid old *George*.

'Not bad,' says Ben. 'The Photoshop stuff is easy—I did that at my old school. But I'm not so good at Flash animation.'

'Oh,' says Tahni with another thousand-watt smile, 'Flash is easy. I'm really good at it, so let me know if you need any help.'

'Thanks,' says Ben, smiling back.

I scowl. How dare she flirt with my boyfriend like that? Isn't there some kind of girl code? That you stay away from your best friend's boyfriend? I know I'm not that experienced in the whole boyfriend-girlfriend-social-politics thing, but I know that what she's doing is not okay.

And he's *smiling* at her! There's no way I can compete with Tahni and her super-curvy-thousand-watt flirtiness.

'It's so unfair,' I say. 'You're in a class together, and I have to be in a class with stupid old Hannibal Lecter.'

'Who?' says Tahni.

'The New Guy,' I say. 'You know. George Papadopoulos.'

Tahni frowns. 'Why did you call him a Lecturer?'

'Lecter,' I say. 'Hannibal Lecter. From *Silence of the Lambs*?'

Tahni looks baffled. She glances at Ben, who shrugs and shakes his head.

'I never know what she's talking about,' he says.

This is really annoying. '*Silence of the Lambs*,' I say. 'You know, that famous old movie about the serial killer who removed people's skin? It had Jodie Foster in it?'

'I'm really not seeing the connection, Midge,' says Tahni. She turns back to Ben. 'So do you have that new FX Photoshop plug-in?'

'Remember you said that stuff about the New Guy being weird and a possible killer at his old school,' I interrupt.

Tahni manages to convey concern and scorn at the same time. 'That's hardly something you should be making jokes about, Midge.'

I sigh. 'Never mind.'

George would have understood the reference. Although he probably wouldn't have thought it was funny, what with it being about him and all.

But then Ben leans over and whispers into my ear, in a low, private voice that is only meant for me.

'Do you have a dollar?' he murmurs.

'A what?' I say, delirious.

'A dollar. I want a Mars Bar, but I don't have enough money.'

'Of course,' I fumble in my pocket. The poor boy. A Mars Bar probably costs twenty-five pence or whatever in England. He has to get used to a new currency as well as a new school and new friends. I am so happy I can help him, it doesn't matter that now I won't have enough money for a pie at lunchtime. I hand over the coin.

'Thanks,' he says. 'See you later.'

He kisses me swiftly, then saunters away.

I watch him go. Who cares about the pie? I will never have to eat again. I am sustained by my love for him. That kiss will keep me going until at least dinnertime.

'He looks so hot in school uniform,' I say to Tahni. 'What is it, about some boys? Most of them look terrible in it, but Ben looks like it's been personally tailored for him.'

'Do you think we could possibly have a conversation about something other than Ben?' says Tahni.

Wow. She just killed those watts like flicking off a light-switch. She's back to grumpy and snide. And how can she say that about Ben after she just turned the full charm offensive on him? She really is testy. It's definitely jealousy. As if I haven't been in exactly the same position, listening to her go on for ever about some Boy she met at Luna Park or Nando's. Man.

'Fine,' I say. 'What do *you* want to talk about then?'

'Actually,' says Tahni, 'I have to go to the library.'

She gets up and walks away. I watch her, stunned. Tahni, go to the library? I bet she doesn't even know where it is.

When I arrive at my History class, I'm feeling guilty about Tahni. I should be more understanding. She's single. Probably lonely. I should be grateful for this opportunity to perfect being empathetic, rather than just plain old pathetic. But by the time I walk out again to go to French, I'm just plain old angry.

She's supposed to be my friend! She should be happy for me. So what if I want to talk about my new boyfriend for five minutes?

I decide to avoid her at lunchtime and seek out Ben instead. I need some kisses to sustain me.

As I make my way down the corridor to his locker, I'm stopped by Nina Kennan. At first I don't think she's actually talking to me, so I look behind to check who else is around. But it is me. Nina Kennan has never spoken to me in my life. Nina Kennan and I have been going to the same school since we were five, and she has never once spoken to me. People like Nina Kennan don't speak to people like me.

Nina is the kind of girl who never would have done anything so unglamorous as be born. She was never a squalling purple creature covered in gunk. She just appeared one day, floating down from the clouds in a pale pink cashmere blanket carried by white doves.

Nina has perfect blonde hair. Perfect blue eyes. A smattering of freckles across her perfect nose. She smells like lily-of-the-valley and has perfectly straight white teeth.

'Midge,' she says, and I'm surprised that her words aren't echoed by a chorus of nightingales.

How does she even know my name?

'Hi, Nina,' I say.

'My parents are going away this weekend,' she says, flicking back her shampoo-commercial hair with a pale and perfect finger. 'I'm having a party. You should come.'

I nearly fall over. She's inviting me to a party?

'Really?' I say. I think of all the times Tahni and I had laughed and giggled and gossiped about Miss Nina Perfect Kennan. I think of how we swore we would never ever be her friend, just because she was so irritatingly perfect. But I don't think either of us imagined it would actually happen.

'Bring whoever you like,' she says, as she turns to go. 'Bring that new boy.'

'So,' says Ben, running his thumb over my wrist as we sit behind the basketball court. 'What's new?'

'Not much,' I say. I think about telling him how weird Tahni's been today, but decide not to. It's sort of because of Ben, and I don't want him to feel bad.

'Who are you doing your English project with?' I ask instead.

'No one,' Ben replies. 'Everyone in my class already has a partner, so I have to do it on my own.'

I ponder the unjust cruelty of the world for a moment. If I were in Ben's class, and he had come to school a day earlier, we could be doing our project together! Instead he has to do it all by himself, and I'm stuck with stupid socks-pulled-up George. I mean sure, George has had some good ideas, and that story about the Care Bear was pretty funny, but he's still a weirdo.

'Have you thought about what you'll do it on?' I ask.

'Do what on?'

'Your project. Do you have any ideas?'

Ben smiles at me, this beautiful, radiant, warm smile. His eyes make me go all gooey inside. Those eyes are just for me.

'I thought I'd get you to do it.'

I'm still drowning in the eyes. 'Hmm?'

'My project. You know how I said I'd think of a way for you to make it up to me? For not telling everyone your secret? I figured you could do my Communication Project and then we'd be square.'

'Oh,' I say. This feels wrong. This isn't the kind of thing that a boyfriend asks his girlfriend to do. Not that I necessarily am his girlfriend. We haven't really discussed it yet. How do you tell? Is it something you have a conversation about?

'I was thinking something to do with the media,' he says. 'Photography maybe. Something cutting-edge.'

I think about that moment in the hallway, when I wanted to die. I wonder what would have happened if Ben hadn't rescued me. He could have laughed, or said he'd never seen me before, and then everyone would know what a sad loser I am.

Except I'm not a sad loser anymore. Overnight, I went from being pathetic Midge Arkles, who's never had a boyfriend and is so desperate she *MADE ONE UP*, to Fabulous Midge Arkles. A Midge Arkles with a hot boy kissing her in the corridors. A Midge Arkles who wags school to go to a cafe with aforementioned hot boy. A Midge Arkles who people are *jealous* of. A Midge Arkles who gets invited to Nina Kennan's party. A Midge Arkles who just might be . . . popular.

And it's thanks to Ben. This change is because of him. And it's not just because he didn't tell everyone I made up an imaginary boyfriend. I *feel* different. The way he looks at me, and talks to me, and nuzzles my neck. It makes me feel like a real girl. It makes me proud to be me. It makes me feel beautiful and special and unique. Because he wants *me*.

So I tell him yes. I'll do his project for him.

We spend the rest of lunchtime kissing. I'm in such a good mood, that, when I see Tahni on my way to Politics, I invite her to Nina's party.

9 **hul·la·ba·loo**

/hʌl'ə-bə-luu'/

–noun; a clamorous or exciting noise or disturbance;
uproar.

– A Wordsmith's Dictionary of Hard-to-spell Words

{ Five things I'd never done before this week: }

1 Kissed a boy for hours until my lips went numb

2 Spoken to Nina Kennan

3 Been to Nina Kennan's house

4 Been to a proper, no grown-ups, lots of beer
party like in American teen movies

5 Drank beer

I'm doing all of them right now. I'm not so crazy about the beer, which tastes like the bottom of a laundry basket, but everything else is fantastic.

I'm sitting on Ben's lap in Nina's living room, and the party is flowing around us. There's music and dancing and lots of people pashing and groping in corners.

Ben and I are the King and Queen of the party. We're sitting on our floral upholstered throne, watching our court whirl by. It's awesome.

*Flashback.* Two hours ago, I am a pathetic quivering mess.

What do I wear to a party? I pull every single thing out of my wardrobe. I try on jeans and skirts and dresses. They all make me look like I'm going to a birthday party where there'll be a clown, lolly-bags and a cake shaped like a fairy.

I end up raiding Mum's old collection of hippie clothes. After much deliberation, I choose a middle-eastern-looking cream and pink lace top, which I wear over a black singlet and jeans. It's . . . different. I almost take it off and start again, but I figure with the clothes available to me, my choices are 'boring' or 'different', and 'different' wins. 'Cool' or 'hot' are not options.

I would have been nervous about dressing for a party anyway, but this is the first time Ben will see me out of school uniform. I don't want him to realise he is going out with boring old Midge who would quite happily wear school uniform on the weekends.

I want him to see interesting, funny, beautiful Midge, with an eclectic dress sense.

So I add a few strings of beads and some dangly earrings from Mum's jewellery box, and a badge from a school excursion that says 'I ♥ Happy Endings'. I try putting on some of Mum's make-up, but the result is absolutely ridiculous. Surely the point of make-up is that you end up looking *better* than you do in your natural state. I end up looking like a hooker. And anyway, I don't want make-up to rub off onto Ben's face while we're kissing. That would be embarrassing to the point of death.

Mum can't decide whether to be proud or concerned that I am going to a Proper Teenage Party.

'Will Nina's parents be there?' she asks.

'Of course,' I lie, hoping Mum won't call and check.

'And boys? Will there be boys?'

'Yes, Mum. There will be boys.'

'And alcohol?'

'I don't think so,' I tell her. 'But if there is, I promise not to drink any. Or get too close to any of the boys. Or get pregnant. Or take drugs, or take lollies from strange men. Or cross the road without looking both ways.'

'Don't be smart, Midge,' Mum says.

'Oh!' I add. 'And I will absolutely eat my greens and my crusts so I grow up big and strong.'

She pushes me out the door and follows me to the car.

'Just promise me you'll be careful,' she says, as we reverse down the driveway.

'I promise, Mum.'

I wonder what she'd do if I told her I intend to kiss my boyfriend all night. Frankly, she'd probably throw a party.

I have a brief and painful memory of the surprise family gathering she organised when I first got my period. She served pink, fizzy drinks in champagne glasses, and made whole-wheat strawberry tarts and a very red tofu casserole. She found a red tablecloth and decorated the house with red balloons and streamers. She also made a mixed tape of songs like *Girl, You'll Be a Woman Soon* and *You Make Me Feel Like A Natural Woman* and that awful *Man, I Feel Like A Woman* song. She drank too much of the pink fizzy stuff and sang and danced and cried and made long, heartfelt speeches while my dad and uncles stared at their shoes and looked like they'd rather stick forks in their eyes. It was the most humiliating and painful way I could possibly have entered adulthood.

When we arrive outside Nina's house, Mum leans over and kisses me on the cheek.

'I'm going into the office,' she says. 'But I'll have my mobile if you need me.'

'The office?' I say. 'It's Saturday night!'

Mum looks away. 'We have a big case coming up next week,' she says. 'Anyway. If you want me to pick you up, just call.'

'I'm going back to Tahni's house afterwards,' I tell her. 'Remember?'

'I know, sweetheart, but if you change your mind, you can call me or Dad at any time of the night. No matter how late or early it is.'

Walking up Nina's driveway is like walking barefoot over coals. Her house is enormous and ancient – all gables and boards and wrought-iron lacework. I feel sick and nervous and shivery. I contemplate throwing up in the bushes, but feel it would probably be rude.

Is Ben already here? Is anyone here yet? Nina said eight o'clock, but does that mean eight o'clock or does it mean eight o'clock is for losers and the party won't really start til after midnight? I wish there was a book for teen-party etiquette. Or a website. Actually, there probably is a website, I just wish I'd thought of looking it up.

I'm not the first person to arrive, but the party is hardly pumping. I sit on a green and pink floral sofa in Nina's lounge room (the fanciest room I've ever been into in my life), and try not to breathe on any of the expensive-looking ornaments, or stare at the ye-olde wallpaper. I feel like I'm in a Jane Austen movie.

I chat a bit with some of Nina's friends [Them: 'Oh God, I love your top!' Me: 'Thanks.' Them: 'It's really (giggle) interesting.' Me: 'That's what I was going for.' Them: (vapid stare)], and eat chips. Nina brings me a plastic cup full of not-very-cold beer, which I gingerly sip. Yech. What's all the fuss about with beer?

Ben arrives at nine-thirty, which must be the Officially Cool Time to arrive, because everyone else arrives then too.

I don't think he sees me on the couch, because he goes straight into the kitchen. I wait for him, but when he doesn't emerge after five minutes, I go to find him. He's leaning against the kitchen bench with a cup of beer in his hand, talking to some kids from our school. He looks easy and comfortable talking to kids he doesn't know – I'd be a shivering awkward mess. I am insanely proud of him.

I put my hand on his arm. 'Hey,' I say.

'Hey princess,' he replies, and wraps an arm around me. I nearly explode with happiness.

'Been working hard on my project?' he asks.

The happiness-explosion dims somewhat. 'Um, yeah,' I say. 'It's going to be about how the media manipulates everything so much that photography is no longer an indicator that something is true.'

I'm about to go on (it's actually really interesting), but Ben is starting to glaze over. He drains his beer and refills it, and we wander over to the couch. I end up on Ben's lap, and we start kissing.

This is what parties are all about. This is what I've been missing. I could do this all night.


It's nearly midnight. Tahni's here, but she's dancing or pashing some boy (I think it's Chris Stitz). She's still funny around me, but we said 'Hi' and talked about the fancy wallpaper.

Ben's talking to some guy sitting next to us about the

difference between soccer and AFL. It's really, really boring, but I'm just enjoying being here. I know that when the guy goes for another drink, Ben and I will make out some more until someone else sits down to chat. It's a routine I've totally settled into.

The music is very loud, so Ben puts his lips right up against my ear to speak. It's lovely feeling his breath whisper against my ear, but we're not talking much. The music's too loud. Ben's lips are actually spending more time attached to my lips. Can your lips go numb from too much kissing? Can you get blisters?

Ben's breath is sweet with the alcohol. Somehow beer tastes better when it's on his lips. I've never drunk alcohol before, except for a glass of Baileys at Christmas, and a sip or two of the pink fizzy stuff at my period party. It's all right, I suppose. I don't think I've had enough to *feel* anything, except for a warm and fuzzy sensation. That might be the kissing, though.

Tahni's certainly had more than enough. She weaves past with a plastic cup in her hand, laughing hysterically.

'Chris!' she yells. 'Give me another hickey!'

I roll my eyes. How immature.

I think she sees me do it, because she backtracks.

'Isn't it a great party?' she says. I'm not sure if she's talking to me or not, because she's looking at Ben. Her voice is too loud, even with the music pumping.

I nod. 'Yeah,' I say.

Ben nods too. 'Rocking,' he says.

He is adorable when he uses English slang. Tahni obviously thinks so too, because she reaches out and tugs his sleeve.

'Why aren't you dancing?' she asks. 'You should be dancing. Dancing is awesome.'

I don't like her touching him. Even if it's only his sleeve. Why is she touching him? What does she want? What if he says yes? What if he dances with Tahni and I'm left alone here on the couch? But Ben laughs, and wraps his arms tighter round my waist.

'Maybe later,' he says.

I want to burst open with joy and pride. Hah! He wants to be here with me, Tahni! Not dancing with you. Put that in your plastic cup and chew on it!

Tahni looks at me for the first time since she stumbled over here, and I'm a little scared by her expression. It's not the kind of face that you point towards your best friend. I squirm. But then she smiles, and it's like clouds racing away and the sun coming out.

'Did you see Nina's bedroom?' she says, giggling. 'She has a *canopy bed*.'

'Really?' I ask. 'What a princess.'

I put my hand on Ben's, and we link our fingers. Tahni's eyes flicker. The clouds return.

'I need another drink,' she says, and wanders away, calling for Chris and his 'magic tongue'. Gross.

Ben and I kiss some more. A popular song comes on, and everyone squeals and rushes to the make-shift dancefloor at the far end of the room. Ben wraps his arms tighter around me.

'You're not going anywhere,' he says.

I have absolutely no desire to go anywhere. I could quite happily stay here for the rest of my life. I could just sit on this fancy floral sofa and pash Ben until the day I die.

Unfortunately, there are some aspects of living that get in the way of pashing. One of them is my bladder. I give Ben a final, parting kiss, and stand up. He pouts.

'I won't be long,' I say.

'Can you get me a refill on your way back?' he asks, holding up his empty plastic cup.

I smile. Ben winks at me.

'Don't get lost,' he says.

As I negotiate my way through the crowd, I feel as though people are looking at me with respect. Even envy. I am a Real Girl with an Actual Boyfriend. I exist. I have scaled the social ladder. And frankly, I like the view from up here.

I climb the stairs to the bathroom. There's a queue. I'm sure there's another bathroom, but I'm afraid to open any doors in case I disturb carnal activity. There are things a girl doesn't need to see. I wonder if Tahni's managed to clobber Chris Stitz over the head and drag him into a private corner yet.

Two people stumble out of the bathroom. Eww. I hope they didn't do anything on the toilet seat.

A small blonde girl ahead of me in the queue (I don't know her, she must go to another school) is looking a little green.

'Are you okay?' I ask.

'Yeah,' she says, swaying a little. 'I'm fine.'

The queue moves forward.

'Do you go to school with Nina?' she asks. She seems to be having trouble focussing on my face.

I tell her I do, and ask her how she knows Nina.

'We do calisthenics together,' she says.

I try not to snort. Tahni and I always laugh at the calisthenics girls. Tahni says they're all called Sharon or Kelly, with long blonde hair in a head-scrapingly tight ponytail, and are only doing calisthenics because they're not bendy enough to do gymnastics.

Right now it looks like this Sharon-Kelly couldn't even walk in a straight line, let alone twirl a baton.

The bathroom door opens, and Sharon-Kelly goes in.

I lean against the wall and wait. I replay the delicious scene when Ben blew Tahni off in my mind. I really don't know why she's being such a cow. I suppose she's jealous.

But she has a new boyfriend every week. Isn't it fair that I get my turn? I've NEVER had a boyfriend before. Maybe she's jealous that mine is better than all of hers put together. But that's what happens when you have standards.

The bathroom door opens, and the Sharon-Kelly comes out. She's looking less green.

'I'm sorry,' she says as she walks past.

I walk into the bathroom.

Sharon-Kelly has thrown up, and she's completely missed the toilet. Actually, it looks like she might have got some in the toilet, because there's vomit on the toilet seat. It is seriously like a scene from that old horror movie where the girl's head spins round and round. Perhaps Sharon-Kelly was practising some kind of Esther Williams-style calisthenics routine, but with vomit instead of water. I am astonished that such a small girl could have so much vomit in her. It *stinks*.

For a moment, I wonder where Nina's mum keeps the cleaning product. I wonder if I can find a mop and some disinfectant. But only for a moment.

Because cleaning up the drunken vomit of some calisthenics girl I met five minutes ago is the kind of thing that Old Midge would do. Boring, responsible Old Midge.

New Midge turns around and walks out.

There's no one queuing behind me, so I saunter down the hallway, and pick a door at random.

Paydirt. It's the master bedroom. There's a moving lump under the covers, but I ignore it and speed past to the ensuite.

Then I pee (relief!), wash my hands, fluff my hair and go back downstairs.

New Midge is confident. New Midge is popular. New Midge is beautiful.

I get Ben another beer, and return to our couch.

Except he isn't there.

My stomach lurches, and I can smell the vomit from the bathroom again. But I tell myself not to be silly. He probably needed to pee, too.

I scout the room to see if he's in the kitchen or coming down the stairs.

I do see him.

But he's not in the kitchen. Or coming down the stairs.

He's dancing.

Dancing with Tahni.

Except I'm not sure if you call what they're doing dancing.

She's has her arms wrapped around him, and is pressing her whole body against him. Her head is on his shoulder, her face towards his neck. Is she *kissing* his neck? She can't be.

I immediately try to assess Ben's body language. Is he enjoying this? Did he choose to dance with her? Did she force him into it? I can't tell. His hands are on her waist, but he could be gently trying to prise her away. He is nothing if not polite, after all. Surely if he was enjoying it, if he wanted to be there, then he'd have his arms around her. He doesn't. His hands rest uncomfortably on her waist.

I stand there, open-mouthed.

How could she do this to me? She's my best friend, and here she is, sleazing onto my boyfriend! We've been friends since kindergarten!

This has to stop. I have to do something. People are looking at me, looking at Tahni and Ben, whispering, nudging. I am being *judged*. I see a girl with *sympathy* on her face. Oh no. Not yet. This isn't over yet. Surely Ben's just being polite. Surely.

I march into the crowd, elbowing people aside. Ben doesn't look particularly shocked or guilty when he sees me – I figure this is a good thing.

'You Australian girls are very friendly,' he says with a lazy smile.

I ignore him, grab Tahni by the shoulders and yank her off Ben. It's like trying to get a limpet off a rock. She clings to him and makes a pathetic drunken moaning noise.

'What do you think you're doing?' I say, shaking her.

When I let go, she immediately tries to attach herself to Ben again. I notice his neck has lipstick on it. Tahni's make-up is smeared all over her face. I pull her away again. Her face twists slowly into a weird combination of hurt and angry and apologetic.

'What?' she slurs. 'What's your problem? We're just having a dance.'

I can't bear to look at her. She is so pathetic.

What happened to the crazy, happy girl who used to make up extra calisthenics competition categories, like Hair-Bleaching and Eye-Squinting and Cat-Fighting?

People are still staring at us. If this was a movie, I'd slap Tahni, and she'd vomit on my shoes.

Tahni shoves her face towards mine. She stinks of alcohol.

'You think you're so perfect,' she says loudly. 'You think that you're all perfect with your perfect family and perfect grades and your spelling and your perfect perfect boy-friend.'

I don't say anything. I want to say *Yes! Yes I do! I do think everything's pretty perfect right now. Until you came along and ruined it all.*

'Well guess what,' Tahni says. I think she's crying. 'Not everything is perfect. Life isn't perfect. I'm not perfect. And I'm sick of being the dumb one. I'm sick of being the funny, stupid sidekick to little miss perfecty-perfect.'

I feel like she's slapped *me* across the face. 'What are you talking about?' I say. 'You do nothing but tease me about how square I am, and how I'll end up lonely with cats.'

As I say this, I'm suddenly aware that I'm surrounded by people. I don't want Ben to hear this. I turn to him to see if he's laughing at me, but he's not there. I can't see him anywhere.

'That was the only thing that was *mine*!' says Tahni. She's really sobbing now, thick full tears that smear down through her eyeliner and mascara, making wet, black trails down her cheeks. 'The one thing you weren't perfect at. The one thing I can do that you can't. And you stole that, too, with your perfect, too-good-to-be-true boyfriend.'

Where *is* my perfect, too-good-to-be-true boyfriend? I'm looking around. I want to find him and get back to the happy, glowing, king-and-queen-of-the-party feeling. This is not my idea of fun.

Tahni glares at me. For a moment I think she's going to say something else, or throw up on my shoes, but she doesn't.

'I need another drink,' she says.

Chris Stitz appears beside her. 'I think you've had enough,' he says.

Tahni slumps against him and presses her face up against his neck. 'Chris,' she says. 'Let's go upstairs. I want another hickey.'

She tries to put her hand down his pants, but he takes it gently and places it on his shoulder. Then he wraps an arm around her, and gives me a sort of wry smile. 'I'll take her home,' he says. 'I've got money for a taxi, and she lives near me.'

I nod.

It's only when he's dragged her from the room that I remember I am supposed to be sleeping over at her house.

I go into the kitchen to find Ben. He's resting against the counter, another beer in his hand, talking to another blonde girl I don't know. He's leaning towards her with his little half-smile.

That's *my* smile! He only looks at *me*, with those warm eyes. She's totally into him – staring up at him through her slutty eyelash implants, playing with her platinum hair extensions. Her skirt is very short. She laughs, and reaches out and touches his arm in an 'Oh, you!' sort of way.

Ben glances up and sees me. He winks at me and mouths *five minutes* and waves me back into the living room.

I am suddenly very out of my depth. I go cold, and start to feel queasy.

The party isn't fun anymore. The music is too loud. There are too many people. They're all drunk and pawing each other like animals. Three girls are doing vodka shots off the coffee table. Another girl is dancing wearing only her bra and undies. Five boys are having a skolling competition in the kitchen. The floral couch is now occupied by a couple who seem to be practically having sex.

My stomach is churning and I can smell the calisthenics vomit from the bathroom. Every time I close my eyes I can see it, splattered all over the floor and the toilet seat. Little chunks of carrot and pasta.

I need fresh air.

I stumble out the front and throw up into the perfectly manicured lavender bushes. I feel like I've come full circle. I should have done it on the way in and saved myself all the bother.

I want to go home.

I find my mobile and check the time. It's 3 am.

Mum did say I could call at any time of the night.

I'm shivering. It's not cold, but I can't stop shaking. I just want to go home.

I dial Mum's mobile number. She answers after three rings, her voice all sleepy and confused.

'Midge?' she says. 'Is everything all right? Are you okay?'

'I'm fine, Mum,' I say. 'Can you come and get me? I want to come home.'

'Of course, sweetheart,' she says. 'I'll be there in ten minutes.'

'I'm sorry it's so late,' I say. I am trying hard not to cry.

'I'll see you soon,' she says, and hangs up.

It's the longest ten minutes of my life. I huddle on Nina's front steps, trying not to cry, and trying not to think about Tahni and Ben and the blonde girls and the party. I'm also trying not to think about the bitter taste of vomit in the back of my throat. I could go inside for water, but the thought of seeing Ben with the eyelash-batting, hair-extension-twirling, arm-touching blonde almost makes me throw up again.

I try to distract myself with spelling difficult words. I try to think of one for every letter of the alphabet. Accommodate. Barbiturate. Camaraderie.

I can't get Tahni's tear-and-make-up-smeared face out of my mind. I can't stop seeing her pressed up against Ben.

Diphtheria. Exacerbate. Furlough.

Ben leaning towards the blonde girl. Vomit all over the bathroom.

Gnarl. Harangue. Intravenous.

I'm nearly at the end of the alphabet (ukulele, vicissitudes, witticise) by the time Mum arrives.

'You're sure you're okay?' she asks.

I nod. 'Sorry to get you out of bed,' I say. Then I notice what she's wearing. 'Why are you wearing work clothes?' I ask. 'Have you been home?'

Mum laughs. 'I fell asleep at the office,' she says. 'With my head on the desk. It's lucky you rang. I might have been there all night.'

I reach forward and turn the heating on full blast.

'Why didn't you go home with Tahni?' Mum asks. 'Did you have a fight?'

I swallow. 'No,' I say. 'She wanted to stay at the party, and I was tired and wanted to go home.'

Mum says nothing. I don't think she believes me.

# 10  re·sid·u·um

/rɪˈzɪdʒuəm/

–noun; the residue, remainder, or aftermath of
  something.

– The Wordsmith's Dictionary of Hard-to-spell Words

I wake up at nine, and shuffle downstairs in my pyjamas. I take Gregory, my bear, with me in case I need him. I fix myself a Milo (equal parts milk and Milo), and two slices of peanut butter toast.

Mum and Dad are nowhere to be seen – I guess they're sleeping in.

I turn on the TV and watch cartoons. They're not as good as I remember them. I wonder what's changed – the cartoon quality or me. Only one way to find out, I suppose. I dig through the DVD cabinet until I find *Toy Story*. I used to love this film when I was little.

I put it in the DVD player. While it loads, I climb the stairs and grab my doona and a pillow.

When Mum comes downstairs at ten-thirty, I'm nearly asleep, with a half-empty packet of chocolate biscuits balanced on my stomach.

'Do you have a hangover?' Mum asks suspiciously.

'No,' I say, and then wonder if I do. I'm pretty sure I'm just tired – I only had half a plastic cup of beer.

'Your period?'

'No, Mum. I'm just tired.'

Mum gives me this funny look, and then climbs under the doona with me.

'I feel like you're growing up fast, and I'm missing out on it because I'm at work all the time,' she says.

'I'm not growing up,' I say.

On the TV, Woody is trapped inside a milk crate in Sid's room.

Woody bleats at Buzz Lightyear despondently. *Why would Andy want to play with me when he's got you?*

I think about the blonde girl talking to Ben in Nina's kitchen.

'Actually,' I say, 'I'm thinking about giving it a miss.'

'Giving what a miss?' Mum helps herself to a biscuit.

'Growing up,' I say. 'I think it's overrated.'

Mum raises her eyebrows.

'It is,' I say. 'You have to get a job, and earn money, and pay bills. And you're not even allowed to watch cartoons anymore, you can only watch Serious French Cinema.'

Mum laughs, and pokes Gregory. 'And you're not allowed to have a teddy bear.'

I give Gregory a squeeze. 'Exactly. Why would I want to do any of that?'

Mum smiles a sad smile. 'You make a good case,' she says.

Buzz is getting all sentimental on the screen, looking at Andy's name written on his foot.

'Dad's sleeping late,' I say.

'He's gone out,' says Mum. 'To visit your grandma.'

Good. That means I don't have to go with him. I hate visiting Grandma. I know that makes me sound like a bad person, but she doesn't remember who I am anyway, and the old people's home smells funny.

'We should go out too,' says Mum.

'To visit Grandma?' I say, my heart sinking. I have plans for *Toy Story 2*.

'No,' says Mum. 'We should have a girls day. Go out for lunch. Go shopping. See a movie.'

I think about this. I'm not entirely sure I'm ready to deal with the outside world. But I'm going to have to leave the house sooner or later, and I'd certainly feel safer if I had my mum with me. And anyway, everyone from the party will be at home today nursing their hangovers.

'Okay,' I say. 'Let's do it.'

'*Yeah!*' says Woody, just before I click off the TV.

We go to our favourite shopping strip, and have lunch at a real restaurant. I have pancakes with maple syrup and bananas and bacon, and Mum doesn't even raise her eyebrows. She has curly fancy pasta with prawns, and a glass of white wine. We talk about school and spelling and her new case at work. She doesn't ask me about the party. I think she knows I don't want to talk about it.

'So tell me more about this project you're doing,' Mum says.

'It's about secrets,' I say. 'We're setting up a website where students can anonymously post their secrets.'

'What kind of secrets?'

I shrug. 'Who they have a crush on. What test they cheated in. How they lied to their parents about something. Usual teenage stuff.'

Mum raises her eyebrows.

'For most teenagers,' I say. 'Normal for most teenagers. Not me. I'm abnormal. No secrets here.'

Mum sips her wine and says nothing.

'We're going to use the site to analyse what issues are important to teenagers today,' I say. 'We figure the things kids keep secret are the things they care most about.'

I wonder if Mum has any secrets. Maybe what I'm getting for my birthday. I guess once you're married and have kids, there's less things to be secretive about, apart from all the Santa, Easter Bunny stuff.

When we leave the restaurant, I think I see Ben on the other side of the road, and nearly bring up my pancakes all over the footpath. But it's not him, it's someone else.

I'm not sure why I'm so nervous about seeing him. It's not like he did anything really wrong. It's not like *he* was the one who yelled at me and tried to hurt me. But I don't want to see him. I don't even want to think about him. Thinking about him makes me remember the way Tahni was touching him, and the expression on her face when she looked at me.

Mum and I go to all the shops. I don't know what's gotten into her, but I make out like a bandit. She buys me a navy blue dress, and these cute red shoes to go with them. It's pretty much the coolest thing I've ever owned, all retro and vintage-looking. Then she buys me a red necklace to match the shoes, and I start to get worried.

'Mum, are you dying?' I ask as we walk out of the jewellery shop.

'What?' says Mum.

I heft my shopping bags. 'All this largesse,' I say. 'Are you buttering me up for some bad news?'

Mum rolls her eyes. 'I'm not dying.'

'What about Dad?'

'Aren't I allowed to spend some time and money on my daughter?'

I'm not convinced.

In the DVD shop, Mum hovers over a special edition of *Breakfast at Tiffany's* while I eye off the latest season of *Grey's Anatomy*.

'So are you contributing one?' asks Mum.

'One what?'

'A secret. Are you submitting a secret to the website?'

I hadn't really thought about it.

'Probably not,' I say.

But I wonder what my secret would be, if I did.

*I made up an imaginary boyfriend.*

*A boy is going out with me in exchange for me doing his homework for him.*

*I don't want to grow up.*


As we walk in the front door, the phone is ringing, and my stomach immediately lurches. I taste the pancakes again. What if it's Ben? What if it's Tahni?

Mum answers it, and then passes the phone to me. 'It's for you,' she says.

I think I'm going to faint.

'Someone called George,' she says.

Oh, George. Thank God for George. I take the phone.

He wants to know when we can work on our project. I'm so incredibly relieved it's him and not Tahni or Ben (or even Nina, complaining about the state of her lavender bushes), that I invite him over right away. He sounds sort of surprised, but says he'll come.

'A boy?' teases Mum. 'You invited a boy to our house?'

I roll my eyes at her. 'It's for a school project,' I say.

'Uh huh.'

'Really, Mum,' I say. 'I'm not interested. You'll understand why when you see him.'


When George arrives I take him up to my bedroom. He looks a bit less dorky in casual clothes, but his jeans are too high-waisted, and make him look lumpier than ever. He's wearing this windcheater that would have been more suitable for a fifty-year-old golfer. His hair still needs product. And while I'm reasonably certain he's wearing his Dunlop Volleys with absolutely no sense of retro irony, I decide to give him the benefit of the doubt.

Thinking like a cool person reminds me of the party and Tahni, so I stop. George doesn't look bad. That's enough. At least I don't have to pretend to be cooler than I am around him. I'm always going to be higher up on the ladder than George, no matter what happens.

George has a small cut above his left eye, and his right wrist is bandaged.

'What happened to you?' I ask.

He looks uncomfortable. 'Nothing,' he says. 'I fell down.'

'You sound like a battered wife,' I say. 'Is there anything you want to talk about?'

He hunches his shoulders. 'It's really nothing,' he says.

'Come on,' I tease. 'You got into a rumble, didn't you?'

He laughs, sort of weakly. 'Yeah,' he says. 'You got me.'

I sit on my bed, rather self-consciously, and he sits on a chair, taking in the posters on my walls, and the books on my bookshelf.

'I love that series,' he says, pointing to a group of battered paperbacks.

'Me too,' I say. 'Obviously.'

I've never had a boy in my bedroom before. I wish I'd hidden all my soft toys in the cupboard. George's biscuity smell is extra strong today, vanilla and sugary.

George reaches into his bag and pulls out a folder. It has a big sparkly sticker of a dragon on the front. I feel myself blushing. I'm embarrassed for him.

'I've drawn up some designs for the site,' he says, opening the folder. He doesn't seem to be embarrassed by the dragon, so I don't know why I am.

'Great,' I say. 'I've got the text all ready to go. We just need to build it.'

'Do you have Dreamweaver?' George asks.

I'm about to say 'No, but Tahni can get it for us,' when I remember that I'm not in a position to be asking Tahni any favours at the moment. Or really, speaking to her at all. So I just shake my head.

'We need to figure out how to publicise it,' says George. 'Flyers?'

I nod. 'And we can put something in the school news-letter.'

'Email?'

'Yep,' I say. 'Oh, and we should run a competition. Contribute to the Secret Project and go into the running to win movie tickets or something.'

'The Secret Project,' George says, smiling. 'I like that. Sounds like a top secret government file.'

I feel strangely proud to have impressed him. So much of this project has been his ideas. At least I came up with the name.

'Like those files that prove that the moon landing was fake,' I say.

George laughs. 'Or that Madonna was assassinated by the Ku Klux Klan in the 80s and was replaced with a robot.'

'Or that Bert Newton is an alien in a rubber mask!'

That really sets George off, and we speculate about which other celebrities are aliens wearing rubber masks.

'What about Oprah?' I say. 'Or Paris Hilton?'

George laughs again. 'So how was the party?' he asks, out of the blue.

Just like that, my nice warm Sunday evening feeling vanishes. It's as though I'm back at Nina's. Tahni is looking at me with cold, make-up-smeared eyes. Ben is talking to that hair-extensions girl. The vomit is splattered all over the bathroom. The floral couch is being deflowered.

I swallow. 'How did you know about the party?' I ask, trying to buy time.

George shrugs. 'Everybody at school was talking about it on Friday.'

'Oh.' I feel guilty that George wasn't invited. But it wasn't my party. Even though Nina said I could bring whoever. I don't think George counts. And he wouldn't have had a good time anyway. Not that I had a good time.

I'm pretty sure George can read my thoughts, because he says, 'I would have gone, but I had other plans.'

I nod. This is a lie, and we both know it. But it makes things easier.

'So?' he says.

I stare at him. I really, really don't want to talk about the party.

'How was it?' he asks again.

'It was okay.'

I pick up his folder and consider his notes. A loose page falls out onto the floor. I reach for it.

'Don't—' says George.

I stare at it. It's a map. It looks like a map from a fantasy novel. Everything's divided up into little octagons, which are all different colours. There's a bunch of red octagons together in the area called 'Eldritch Swamplands'. There's an even bigger blue section in the 'Forests of Rangokk'. The biggest section is yellow, which stretches from the 'Hollow Mountains' to the 'Simikk Plains'.

George snatches it out of my hands.

'Is this from a book?' I say.

'It's nothing,' he says, folding the map and stuffing it in his pocket.

'What is it? A map to buried treasure?'

George waves a hand at his folder, which is still on my lap. 'We should get started on writing this proposal.'

I narrow my eyes. 'Come on, tell me what it was.'

He looks so awkward, I think he might fall apart. 'It's really not important,' he says. 'We have work to do.'

'It *is* important,' I say. 'We're doing a project about secrets. And you seem to have one.'

I think I might be flirting with George. This is very strange.

'Come on,' I plead. 'Tell me.'

'Tell me about the party.'

Checkmate.

Now it's my turn to squirm. 'It was fine,' I say. 'You know, just a party.'

George raises his eyebrows and his forehead does the crinkly thing it does. 'So you didn't have a good time.'

'Sure I did,' I say, without much enthusiasm.

'Did you and Mister Perfect have a fight?' asks George.

He knows about me and Ben. For a moment I feel quite proud – king and queen of the school again. But the feeling doesn't last long.

'No,' I say, but I'm not sure if that's true.

'Then what?'

What is this, the Spanish Inquisition?

'I sort of had a fight with Tahni.' I'm surprised that I say it. To George of all people. I really don't want to talk about it, but it all comes spilling out.

'Ever since Ben arrived, she's been weird,' I say. 'It's like I'm not allowed to have a boyfriend. She just wants to keep me in my little box where she can bring me out and play with me when she wants to. I'm not allowed to have a life of my own. Boys are her territory. I'm just there to be teased for not having one.'

I stop. I'm coming dangerously close to talking about the whole Imaginary Boyfriend thing.

'Why are you friends with her?' George asks.

I shrug. 'We've always been friends,' I say. 'Since kinder.'

'So, you're just friends out of habit?' he says.

'No,' I say. 'She's fun. She's always thinking up exciting

things to do. Like when we went snorkelling in the fountain outside the Art Gallery. Or when we dressed up in our mums' fancy dresses and crashed a wedding in the Fitzroy Gardens.'

'But is she a good friend?' asks George.

'What do you mean?'

'What's she like when you're not having fun? When you're sad?'

I think about this. 'She bought me a Snickers bar when I failed a Maths test last year,' I say. 'And when I had tonsillitis in Year 7 she came over each day after school and told me what I'd missed.' I smile. She wrote me a letter in every class, and tied them with a pink ribbon for me to read the next day. 'She's a good friend,' I say. 'Or at least she was.'

'What was the fight about?'

'I don't know,' I say. 'She was really drunk, and she wanted to dance with Ben. She was all over him, and I got angry—'

I stop because I honestly think I might cry or throw up.

'So she's jealous,' George says.

'But that's not fair!' I say, my voice going wobbly. 'She has a new boyfriend every five minutes!'

George smiles his serious smile. 'Don't you think that's why she's jealous?'

'What?'

'Why do you think she has a new boyfriend every five minutes?' he asks.

I shrug.

'Maybe,' says George gently, 'Maybe it's because she hasn't found the right one? And so she's trying and trying to find one she has a connection with, and you stroll in and find the perfect boy on the first go.'

I hadn't thought about it that way. I frown at George. 'Are you gay?' I ask.

'What?'

'It's no big deal if you are,' I say. 'You just seem awfully perceptive for a boy.'

He laughs. 'I'm not gay.'

I'm not sure I believe him.

'Can I ask you something?' George says. 'When Tahni was "all over" Ben – what did he do?'

I think about Ben's hands on Tahni's waist.

'Did he blow her off?' asks George.

'No-o,' I say. 'He didn't want to hurt her feelings.'

'So he hurt yours instead.'

'It wasn't like that,' I say.

'But he danced with her.'

'Yes, but he didn't want to.'

George makes a skeptical face. 'And he told you that.'

I bite my lip.

'Sounds like a really nice guy, your Mister Perfect,' says George.

I think about Ben leaning towards the blonde girl with his special half-smile. I swallow.

'He *is* nice,' I say. 'He *is* perfect. You don't understand.'

'Understand what?' George says. 'That he's a player?'

'You don't know what he's done for me,' I say. I think about what would have happened if Ben hadn't kept my secret. Who cares if he was talking to some girl? He's allowed to talk to other girls. I talk to other boys. There's a boy in my freaking bedroom! Doesn't mean I want to pash him (shudder). I'm turning into one of those creepy over-protective girlfriends who deletes girls' phone numbers from their boyfriends' mobile. I need to chill. Ben wouldn't have kept my secret if he didn't like me. He wouldn't have spent almost all of the party kissing me on the couch. He wouldn't look at me the way he does if he didn't feel the same way I do.

'I don't expect you to understand,' I say to George. 'Relationships are complicated.'

'Why wouldn't I understand?'

I don't want to say this, but I do anyway. 'It's obvious you've never had a girlfriend,' I say. 'You're too much of a weirdo.'

George's lips go very thin. 'Of course it is,' he says. 'Obvious.'

He reaches over and takes his folder. 'I should go,' he says.

'George,' I say. 'Wait. I'm sorry. That came out the wrong way.'

'No it didn't,' he says, smiling a self-deprecating smile. 'I appreciate your honesty.'

'Don't go,' I say. 'We still have work to do on the Secret Project.'

He shrugs on his backpack. 'My mum is expecting me home for dinner,' he says.

I tell Mum I'm not feeling well and go to bed before dinner. This has been the worst weekend of my entire life. I can't imagine how it can get any worse than this. I realise that having a good long cry might make me feel better, but I can't do it. There aren't any tears. I'm tired and empty and more than anything I just want to be asleep.

I wake up at 3 am, starving. I tiptoe downstairs.

As I'm walking through the darkened lounge room, I hear noises in the kitchen. The door is ajar, and the kitchen light is on. It's a strange, sniffling, choking sound. Our old dog used to sound like that just before he threw up.

I peer around the kitchen door.

It's Dad. He has a cup of tea in front of him, and his shoulders are shaking up and down and he's making this strange, gasping, gulping noise.

I wonder if it's Grandma. Maybe she's dead. I suddenly feel guilty for not visiting her.

I'm about to say something, but Dad looks so weird. I've never seen him cry before. Parents aren't supposed to cry. They're not supposed to have emotions, apart from anger, disappointment and pride. And fatigue. But they're never supposed to *cry*. It seems like such a personal, private thing. I wonder why he's crying down here. Why isn't he crying in the bedroom where Mum can comfort him? Does he think it's not manly to cry? Is he embarrassed?

Maybe he hasn't told Mum about Grandma. Maybe he's trying to figure out how to tell her. And me.

I feel cold and sick, a bit like I did last night at the party.

It's scary seeing Dad cry.

I sneak back upstairs and slide into bed. I squeeze Gregory tight. I don't want to turn the light off. I'm far too old to be scared of the dark, but all of a sudden I want to be a kid again. The party, Ben, Tahni. Mum acting strange. Dad crying.

Life used to be so much simpler.

# 11 re·cal·ci·trant

/rɪˈkælsɪtrənt/

–adjective; resisting authority; not obedient;
   rebellious.

– The Wordsmith's Dictionary of Hard-to-spell Words

The next morning I go downstairs with my face composed.
I wonder what I should do when they tell me Grandma's
dead. Should I act surprised? Should I cry? I'm not sure if
I can cry, now that I already know.

Dad's sitting at the breakfast table, in almost exactly the
same position as he was last night. Except now there is a
newspaper spread on the table, and he's wearing a suit and
has a bowl of muesli in front of him.

'Hi, Dad,' I say.

He looks up and smiles. 'Morning, chicken,' he says, then
goes back to his newspaper.

I open the fridge and fossick around for the orange juice,
waiting for him to tell me.

He turns a page of the newspaper.

I pour a glass of orange juice, and pull out last night's
leftover curry and start to eat it cold.

Dad makes a face. Here it comes. 'Midge, that smells revolting,' he says. 'I don't know how you can eat that stuff so early in the morning.'

Maybe he's softening the blow. Maybe he doesn't want to tell me before school.

I can't stand the pressure.

'How was Grandma yesterday?'

Dad shrugs. 'Oh, you know your grandmother,' he says. 'In her own happy little world. She asked me if I'd come to deliver the new bookshelves. Then she told me a story about when she used to live in Scotland.'

'Grandma lived in Scotland?'

'Of course she didn't,' says Dad. 'She's never left Australia.'

'Oh.' I put the rest of the curry back in the fridge. 'So she's all right, then? Healthy?'

'As a horse,' says Dad. 'I think she'll outlive us all.'

This is weird. Surely Dad wouldn't lie to me about her being dead. But if she's not dead, then what was he crying about last night?


I get to school just as the bell rings, so I hurry to form assembly without going to my locker first. I try to convince myself that it's because I missed the tram, but actually it's because I don't want to run into Tahni. Or Ben. I don't really want to see George, either, but we're in the same form, so I can't avoid him.

Except it seems like I can, because he studiously ignores

me throughout form assembly, and then runs off as soon as the first period bell rings. I'm ridiculously glad, because it means I don't have to confront the fact that's been churning at the back of my mind since last night. The terrible truth that George was right about Ben.

As I make my way from form assembly to History, I run into Nina Kennan.

'Great party, hey?' she says. 'I was so wasted.'

'Yeah,' I say. 'Wasted.'

'Have you seen Tahni?'

I shake my head and feel guilty.

'She must still be sick.' Nina leans towards me conspiratorially. 'I heard her mum took her to hospital. After Chris dropped her home.'

'Hospital?'

'She got her stomach pumped. Alcohol poisoning.'

'Oh no,' I say. I remember her, stumbling away with Chris Stitz. 'I didn't realise she was that drunk.'

Nina winks at me. 'I'm sure you had other things on your mind,' she says with a smile. 'Like that gorgeous man of yours.'

I ignore this. 'She really had her stomach pumped? You're sure?'

I swallow. It wasn't my fault. Tahni's a big girl. She should have known better than to drink so much. And it still doesn't excuse her behaviour.

'Yep,' says Nina. 'I had to have it done last New Year's. They force a tube down your throat and put charcoal in your stomach. The charcoal soaks up the alcohol and makes you vomit up all this black stuff.'

Make her stop. I don't want to be here. I don't want to think about Tahni with a tube in her throat.

'I have to go,' I say. 'I have a . . . a thing. See you.'

I flee, feeling like the lowliest, most hateful and awfullest creature in the world.


I don't listen in History. Not even when Mr Loriot misspells *goverment*, *disemmination* and *reccurrance*. I can't stop thinking about Tahni, lying in hospital with charcoal smeared around her mouth, the same way that eyeliner was smeared around her eyes at the party. I think about what George said.

*Maybe it's because she hasn't found the right one? And so she's trying and trying to find one she has a connection with, and you stroll in and find the perfect boy on the first go.*

But did I?

I think about Ben dancing with Tahni. And talking to the blonde girl in the kitchen. I think about all the times he called me on the phone or hung out with me. I think about him kissing me. I think about Imaginary Ben. He wouldn't have got me to keep doing his MySpace page. He would have done his own English project. He wouldn't hit me up every recess for a dollar to buy a Mars Bar.

When the bell goes, I wander out in a daze and shuffle towards my locker.

I feel hands on my waist and turn. It's Ben. He leans in to kiss me, and I pull away. I don't know why, but I don't want him to touch me. Every thing I ever found adorable about him now seems sleazy and repulsive. His perfect-fitting uniform and perfect floppy hair are annoying. How much time does he spend in front of the mirror every morning getting it to look like that?

'Did you get my email?' Ben asks. He doesn't appear to notice my repulsion. 'I've got a few more suggestions for my project.'

He doesn't ask what happened to me at the party. He probably didn't even notice I'd gone.

I take a deep breath. 'We need to talk,' I say. 'In private.'

I drag him into an empty classroom. Ben smirks and reaches towards me.

'I like the way you think,' he says, pulling me towards him and leaning down to kiss me again.

I pull away. He raises his perfect eyebrows. I wonder if he plucks them. 'What's your problem?' he asks.

I edge away until there is a table between us. 'This has to stop,' I say.

'What does?'

'This. You. Me. Us. It's over, okay?'

Ben laughs. 'Do you have your period?'

I shake my head. 'Just stay away from me.'

Ben stops laughing. 'What's your problem?' he asks again. 'You wanted the perfect boyfriend. That's what you got. So what's with all the angst?'

I feel as if I'm split in two. A part of me is absolutely disgusted by him, and at myself for letting him use me. But another part is remembering how special I felt when we kissed on the couch at the party. How proud I felt to walk down the hall at school holding his hand. How I loved the sound of his English accent tickling my ear over the phone.

'That blonde girl,' I say. 'The one you were talking to at the party.'

'What about her?'

'Did you kiss her?'

Ben shrugs. 'You left.'

'You cheated on me.'

He snorts. 'I'm not sure you can call it cheating when we're not really going out. It's just pretend, remember?'

'Yeah,' I say. 'I remember. And I don't want to pretend anymore.'

'Whatever,' says Ben. 'It was getting boring anyway. Just make sure my project is done on time and we're even.'

'What?' I say, incredulous. 'I'm not doing your project. It's over, Ben. The deal is off.'

Ben hesitates for a moment, looking at me carefully. 'Are you sure?' he says. 'You realise that means I'll tell everyone the truth.'

I swallow. 'Fine.'

'Everyone will know about how you made up an imaginary boyfriend and then bribed me to pretend to be him.'

'I don't care,' I say. 'I just want this to be over.'

He shrugs. 'Fine. But you'll regret it.'

As he turns to the door to go back into the corridor, it sort of bangs, like someone had been holding it ajar and let go.

Was someone listening?

## 12   as·suage

/əˈsweɪdʒ/

–verb; to make milder or less severe; relieve; ease;
    mitigate: to assuage one's guilt; to assuage
    one's pain.

– The Wordsmith's Dictionary of Hard-to-spell Words

The rest of the school day passes without excitement. Ben doesn't run around the school telling everyone what a loser I am. Maybe he won't.

I hope he won't. I know I said that I didn't care. But of course I do. I don't want to be immortalised as the crazy girl who bribed some guy to be her boyfriend.

Ben isn't really a bad person. I'm sure he won't say anything. Anyway, it'd reflect badly on him too. Destroy his image of perfection.

I see Tahni in the distance a couple of times during school. She looks pale and quiet.

I want to talk to her – tell her I'm sorry for being such a bad friend. But I'm scared she hates me.

It takes me a whole week to pluck up enough courage to act. I've been hiding in the library at recess and lunch.

Tahni's not talking to me. I'm not talking to Ben. The only person I've spoken to (excluding parents and teachers) is George. And even he's acting a bit strange – I suppose he's still upset that I called him a weirdo.

I feel bad – but really, he's blowing this out of proportion. So I called him a weirdo – he *is* a weirdo! He should embrace it! Be proud of his weirdo-ness. I remember what Tahni said about him getting kicked out of his old school for putting a kid in hospital and stashing pictures of weapons in his locker. I remember the bandage on his wrist and wonder if it could be true.

Still, we've done some productive work on our project and the Secret Project website is up and running. Now we just have to wait for people to submit their secrets.

I miss Tahni. I'm sitting in the library, gathering every scrap of courage I have. But I'm a coward, because I don't have enough courage to actually *talk* to her or even call her. So I send her a text message.

**Sorry 4 everything.**

I spend the rest of my lunchbreak staring at my phone, waiting for a reply.

I remember when Tahni and I first got mobile phones, in Year 7. We used to text each other in class, and at recess when we were sitting together. We kept each other updated every single minute, with dumb messages like 'walking home' and 'nothing in fridge' and 'tofu for dinner' and 'homework sucks'.

When Mum got my first phone bill, she went ballistic. It was over $200. Tahni and I were both grounded, and had our phones confiscated. It took us six months of pocket money to pay off the bills. Six months without chocolate. And we were changed over to prepaid phones, instead of monthly plans.

By the end of lunch, there's still no reply. I wonder if she'll ever forgive me. I think of dumb things I could do, like serenading outside her bedroom window, or sending her a yellow rose every day for the next month.

I leave my phone on for Maths and History. Getting a text from Tahni would be worth a detention.

I slip my hand into my pocket and feel the hard curves of my mobile. I make a silent deal with the universe: I can get a detention, George can keep being cold and distant, as long as I can have Tahni back.

The universe must be listening, because as the final bell rings, my phone beeps along with it.

**No worrys old freind. Talk 2nite.**

I am so happy that I barely notice Tahni's appalling spelling. As I walk home from school, I feel like a weight has been lifted from my shoulders. I am a single girl once more. I never thought being single would feel so good. Tahni has forgiven me. Ben is gone. Everything will be all right now.

There're no enticing cooking smells at home, but I suppose I can't have everything. I go upstairs and check the Secret Project. Three new secrets!

*I lied when I said my mum wouldn't let me sleep over at your house — it's really because I can't sleep without my toy bunny.*

*I know I'm supposed to be supportive, but you can't sing.*

*It wasn't drugs. It was oregano.*

I send George an email. *The project is working!* At five-thirty the doorbell rings. It's Tahni.

I thought she'd look different. Even though it was a whole week ago that she went to hospital. But she looks just like normal Tahni. She smiles and we hug and everything is okay again.

'Let's go to your room,' she says. 'I've got something *amazing* to tell you.'

It's weird, but we don't talk about what happened. I don't mention Ben, and she doesn't mention the party or going to hospital. I suppose it's better that way. We know each other so well, we don't need to go into it all. There are some things that just don't need to be said.

We talk about school, and how Mr Loriot can't spell, and how Mrs Green's spitting-while-talking problem seems to be getting worse. Tahni tells me about this new computer program she downloaded that 'removes noise' from photos. I'm not really sure how a picture can be noisy, but I go along with it.

It feels so good and comfortable to be hanging out with Tahni again. I didn't realise how much I missed her.

We haven't really hung out since last year, before she went to Queensland for the summer holidays. Since she got back, I've been too busy with the two Bens – imaginary and real.

'So what's the big amazing thing?' I ask.

Tahni takes a deep breath, and puts her hands palms-down on my bedspread. 'O.M.G.' she says. Her eyes are shining with excitement. 'You will simply never believe it.'

I laugh, she's so excited. 'Go on,' I say.

'It's the New Guy,' she says. 'I found out his secret.'

I think about the Secret Project and remember how Mum asked me if I was submitting a secret. Is George?

'What secret?' I ask.

'He's not a serial killer,' she says. 'Or a spy or a drug dealer. He's a . . .' words seem to fail her for a moment. 'He's a straight-up honest-to-God *freakazoid*.'

I'm sitting in the same chair George was sitting in last night. I was sitting on the bed where Tahni is now when I called him a weirdo.

'What do you mean?'

'Well,' says Tahni. 'When I was in hospital on Saturday night, he was there too.'

I feel uncomfortable that our silent pact not to talk about the hospital/party thing has been broken.

'I was pretty out of it at first,' says Tahni. 'But later on I was in this recovery ward, with a curtain around my bed because . . . you know . . . charcoal is pretty gross once it's been through your stomach.'

The uncomfortableness settles in for a good long stay.

'Anyway, so I'm lying there, waiting, in case any more comes up, and because they need to observe you for a few hours before they can send you home. And I hear this doctor talking to a patient in the next bed.'

I try not to think of Tahni lying in a hospital bed, waiting to vomit up more slippery black charcoal. It doesn't seem to bother her, though. She's still as bright and shiny as a button.

'And the doctor says this really crazy thing. He says, "If I were you, I'd hold off from the jousting for a few weeks. And maybe in the future you could avoid getting into fights with dragons." And I think, *ce qui*? Dragons? Jousting? What kind of hospital is this? So I peek out from behind my curtain, and there's this guy sitting on the hospital bed wearing a fricking *suit of armour*, for serious. It's not a very good one, it looks all homemade and it's got great big dings in it and the guy doesn't look anything like Viggo in *Lord of the Rings*. But it's still a *suit of armour*. And there's a spear or something leaning against the bed. It was seriously freakish!'

She laughs, and I laugh with her. It does sound crazy.

'So, for a moment I think I'm either still drunk, or they put something in my charcoal and I'm hallucinating. But there really is a knight sitting on a hospital bed, getting his wrist bandaged.'

I suddenly realise where this is going, and feel strange.

'Anyway, he turns his head to the side, and for the first

time I see his face. And I seriously nearly fall out of my bed.'

'Who was it?' I ask, even though I already know.

'New Guy! He thinks he's a knight. New Guy dresses up in armour, and pretends to fight dragons. He's a psycho.'

Tahni flops down onto her back and laughs so hard I'm afraid she'll start throwing up charcoal again.

'Maybe he's in a play?' I say.

'He was covered in mud,' Tahni replies. 'He'd definitely been outside.'

'I'm sure there's a good reason for it,' I say, although I can't think of one. But I know George isn't crazy. He's strange, but he isn't crazy.

Tahni sits up and rolls her eyes at me. 'Don't be lame, Midge,' she says. 'I know you're doing your project with him, but you don't need to stick up for him. He's a freakazoid. End of story.'

'He isn't a freak,' I say.

What am I doing? Why am I sticking up for George? What happened to my deal with the universe?

I just can't help thinking that if we hadn't talked last night about the party, Tahni and I'd still be fighting.

'What's wrong, Midge?' asks Tahni. 'Do you *like* him or something?'

'Of course not,' I say. 'But he's okay. He's not a freak. He's just a bit weird.'

Tahni raises her eyebrows. 'You *do* like him,' she says. 'You *love* him.'

'I don't,' I say. 'Not all of us fall in love with every single boy that we clap eyes on.'

Oops.

Tahni's lips go thin and pinched. 'Right,' she says. 'Sorry, I slipped out of character there, for a moment. It's so hard to remember sometimes. But *I'm* the slutty one, right? And you're the perfect one who knows everything.'

I sigh. This isn't what I imagined at all.

'It's a shame, really,' Tahni continues, shaking her head. 'It's a shame you don't like George. You'd make a lovely couple. Two freaks. Maybe with you helping, he could pretend his way up to a better suit of armour.'

I don't say anything.

'What will Ben say?' Tahni gasps theatrically. 'You'll break his heart.'

I realise she doesn't know that I ended it with Ben. This would probably be a good time to tell her, but I don't. I'm really angry with Tahni. I didn't want to fight with her. I didn't. So why is she being such a cow? And why am I sticking up for George? The universe hates me.

'Oh well, never mind about Ben. You and George will be so romantic together,' says Tahni. 'You can sit around on cold wintry days, holding hands, pretending things together. Because that's what you're really good at, isn't it, Midge? Pretending?'

I don't like the turn this conversation has taken at all. 'I think you're still sick,' I say to Tahni. 'You'd better go home.'

She ignores me. '*Pretending* you're so perfect,' she says. '*Pretending* that everything's okay. *Pretending* to care about anyone else in your life other than yourself.'

She stands up.

'I'm done,' she says. 'I'm sick of pretending.'

And she leaves.

Later that night, I finally get hungry, and go downstairs. It's dark. Mum and Dad don't seem to be home. I'm fixing myself some two-minute noodles when Dad rings.

It's hard to hear him — there's music and loud voices in the background.

'I've got to work late,' he says.

It doesn't sound like he's working. It sounds like he's at the pub. I can hear glasses clinking.

'Where's Mum?' I ask.

I hear the sound of men cheering drunkenly. 'She's gone away for a few days,' says Dad. 'Work stuff.'

'Oh,' I say. That's odd. Why didn't she tell me?

## 13  cat·a·clysm
/ˈkætəˌklɪzəm/

–noun; any violent upheaval, esp. one of a social or political nature.

– The Wordsmith's Dictionary of Hard-to-spell Words

The worst day of my life starts badly, and only gets worse.

I wake up hungry and cranky. Dad's not up yet, and I s'pose Mum's . . . I don't know where Mum is. Working somewhere, I guess. Since when did lawyers have to go away for work? Aren't they chained to their desks?

What if Mum hasn't gone away for work? What if she's been hit by a car and is in a coma? What if she's been kidnapped by the Russian Mafia? What if she's *in* the Russian Mafia and was just *pretending* to be my mother, and has gone home to her Russian family? I bet her Russian daughter Svetlana wouldn't make up an imaginary boyfriend and then break up with him. I bet Svetlana's best friend is still speaking to her.

I'm not sure what time Dad got home last night. I didn't hear him come in, so it must have been pretty late. But his coat's hanging in the hall, so he must have come home eventually. His coat stinks of cigarette smoke. Mum's going to kill him.

Because of the hungry and the cranky, I don't watch the clock while I eat breakfast, and before I know it, it's eight twenty-five, and I'm going to be late.

If Mum were here, I could ask her to drive me. But she's not. And if the smell of Dad's coat is anything to go by, I don't reckon he could legally drive. So I run.

I don't bother brushing my hair or my teeth. I knock over my Milo glass as I race out of the kitchen. It smashes on the kitchen floor, splashing brown chocolate milk onto my white school socks. Crap. I look at the broken glass and milk, knowing that Mum'll freak when she sees it.

But I'll get a detention if I'm late.

And Mum's not here, anyway. Dad can clean it up. Serves him right for being out on the town while his poor daughter starves in a cold, lonely attic.

I run out the front door, and down the street, shrugging my blazer and backpack on as I go.

By the time I reach the street where school is, I am dying of exhaustion. I suspect this is what it feels like to have a heart attack. I'm all sweaty and my hair is sticking to my forehead. My school dress is clammy and unpleasant. The first bell rings, but I can't run anymore. I'll be late to form assembly.

I push open the door, expecting the hall to be empty. It

isn't. It's packed with kids, all yelling, laughing and squealing, their eyes wide and faces flushed.

What's going on? Did something happen? Has school been cancelled? Does the canteen have a half-price dough-nut sale?

Teachers are running around, their arms full of . . . posters? They all have sticky tape trailing off them, so it looks like they've torn them down. Ooh, a scandal. I love a scandal. I step into the hallway, and the door bangs shut behind me.

The hall suddenly goes very, very silent.

It takes me a moment to realise why.

They are all staring at me. I feel like the guy in those old Westerns. The one who enters the saloon and everyone stops drinking and puts down their cards, and the guy with the silly moustache stops playing the piano, and even the monkey (or parrot) drops its banana (or cracker) to stare.

Is it because of the Milo on my socks? I wonder what I must look like – sweaty and puffed, messy hair, brown socks, un-ironed dress. I probably have a Milo moustache as well.

And then I see it.

And I realise that I am at the beginning of the very worst day of my life. Past or future. Nothing will ever be this bad.

The whole school is plastered with posters. Posters of me and George. Well, it's not exactly me and George, because I don't have breasts that big, and I'm pretty sure George doesn't have a piercing . . . there. And we've certainly never been in the same room, at the same time, naked, doing what we're doing in this picture. But it's totally our faces.

The teachers are ripping the posters off lockers. The students all stare at me. Then someone whispers. A titter.

I want to die.

I look around for Tahni or *someone* who will stick up for me. And I see Ben.

He smirks and leans in towards me. 'It's great you've moved on, Midge,' he says. 'I'm glad. I hope we can still be friends.'

I remember him slouching on a table in the empty classroom. What was it he said? Oh yes. *You'll regret it.*

Oh. He did this. Ben did this.

I open my mouth, praying that by some kind of divine miracle, a perfectly witty and biting and face-saving comment will emerge, cutting Ben down where he stands and saving my reputation, and, by extension, my life.

It doesn't. Instead, I stand with my mouth open for a moment, like a fish.

At least, *I* thought it was like a fish.

'Ah,' says Ben, feigning discomfort. 'Not in front of all these people.' He glances at one of the posters. 'I know you're into the exhibitionist stuff, but it's just not my thing. Call me an old romantic.' He grins and makes a suggestive jerk with his eyebrows. 'Maybe later, though.'

And walks off. The titters get louder. Kids are openly laughing at me. My mouth is still hanging open.

I take a deep breath, and exercise the only option left available to me.

I burst into tears.

I gulp and gasp as tears pour down my face. I dread to think what kind of horrible shade of red I've gone. Snot dribbles from my nose.

And everyone turns and walks away.

I stand in the middle of the hallway sobbing and gulping as my fellow students move around me, not making eye contact.

I see Nina Kennan, looking like she just floated in on a sunbeam. I sniffle and hiccup and try to smile.

She looks at me like I am a smear of squished insect on a car windscreen. Something tiny and distasteful, that needs to be discreetly removed as soon as possible.

Mr Mehmet approaches. My embarrassment meter is hovering at eleven. He looks mildly frightened, as if I might start having a fit and he'd have to put a wooden spoon between my teeth. Or as if I already am having a fit, and I might get violent if he gets too close.

'Midge?' he asks. I swallow and try to stop blubbering.

Mr Mehmet places a hand tentatively on my shoulder. 'I think you should come to the Principal's office.'

I don't say anything. I don't really care. My life is over. Nothing could possibly make this worse.

He steers me down the corridor, and I stop outside the computer lab and stare. The embarrassment meter explodes in a shower of tiny glass fragments.

Every single computer is showing the picture of me and George. Except, on the computer screens, it isn't just a picture. It's a weird, disgusting, jerky animation, looped over and over again. I am in a porno. There is a porno of me on every monitor in the computer lab.

'It's on all the school computers,' says Mr Mehmet. 'We can't get rid of it. Someone's hacked into the system.'

Okay, so things can get worse.

George is already in Mr Moss's office. He looks pale.

The bandage on his arm reminds me about what Tahni said last night, about the armour and the lance. Oh. My. God. I am all over the school. In a porno film. With someone who dresses up as a knight and pretends to kill dragons. I hiccup, and burst into tears again.

'Sit down, Midge,' says Mr Moss.

Mr Moss is a very small man. He almost vanishes behind the fancy wooden desk. I wonder if he needs a special chair.

He used to be a Maths teacher, but retired when he went into a diabetic coma in front of his Year 12 Specialist Maths class. He came back to work six months later, and they made him Principal. The secondary school system – it's poetry in motion.

'So,' he says, passing me a box of tissues. 'Do either of you have an explanation for this? Do you know who did it?'

George shakes his head. 'No, sir.'

I busy myself with a tissue.

'Midge?' asks Mr Moss.

'Yes, sir?'

'Do you know who did this?'

'No, sir.'

I'm not sure why I'm lying. I might be able to blame it on being over-emotional, but I know that's not it. In fact, when I take a deep breath, I realise I'm scared.

I mean, if Ben could do this, if he could do something this terrible, what else is he capable of?

I just want it to be over. I want the universe to implode and take everyone's secrets with it. I want to go home and watch *Toy Story* again under my doona with Gregory. I want to run away and become a circus freak (I've already got the freak part down pat). I want to become a nun. I want Mum to come home.

Mr Moss sighs. I'm sure he knows I'm lying.

'Now, I'm confident neither one of you created this . . . this filth. Do you have any idea who might want to hurt you? Someone with a grudge?' He's looking at George when he asks this question.

George is suddenly fascinated with his knees. 'No, sir.'

'I know that there was an . . . incident,' says Mr Moss. 'At your old school.'

What kind of incident? I glance over at George. His face goes a funny colour, but he doesn't say anything. I remember what Tahni said about the locker and the weapons. Maybe he *is* a killer. Maybe he speared someone with his lance.

'Fine,' says Mr Moss. 'The teachers have removed most of the posters, but we haven't been able to fix the computers yet. I think it's probably best if you both went home. I'll call your parents to let them know.'

Great. My parents get to share in my humiliation.

Mr Moss picks up a manila folder and reads the contents. After a moment, George and I realise that this means our meeting is over, and we scurry out of the room.

Thankfully, the corridors are deserted. The posters are all gone, but there're still little paper corners and bits of sticky tape where they've been ripped down. I stare straight ahead when I walk past the computer lab.

'Midge,' George calls.

I spin around. 'Shh!' I whisper. 'People will hear.'

I *so* don't want to be seen with him right now. Actually, I'd be happy if I never saw George Papadopoulos ever again.

'Wait,' he says, and jogs to catch up. He runs like a sack of flour on legs, and wobbles in a rather unfortunate way. I hate him.

I speed to the front door and step outside. It's quite cold, and starting to spit. So much for summer.

'Don't worry,' says George, as we walk out through the school gates. 'It's clear they're fakes. Nobody really thinks we're . . . that we did that.'

I close my eyes and pray that no one can see us together. I imagine every student in the school, pressed up against their classroom windows, whistling and jeering as the porn stars slip off together for another session.

'Do you think it was Ben?' asks George.

I open my eyes in surprise. Why would he say that? How does he even know that we 'broke up'?

George must see my panic, because he frowns and then explains. 'I thought he might be jealous,' he says. 'Because you and I are spending time together.'

'Only because of the project,' I say. I don't want him to think we're friends. That would be Awkward.

George's frown deepens. 'Of course,' he says.

Looks like it's Awkward already. 'We broke up,' I say. 'Ben and I. About a week ago.'

He doesn't look particularly surprised, but I suppose he didn't have much invested in the relationship. 'So do you think he did it?'

I shrug. 'I don't know,' I say. 'Yes. No. Maybe.'

'Why didn't you say anything to Mr Moss?'

'I don't want to make things worse,' I say. 'I don't know what he's capable of.'

George sighs.

I press my palms against my eyes. 'What are we going to do?'

'Just get on with our project,' he says. 'There isn't anything we can do, if you're not willing to tell Mr Moss about Ben.'

I shake my head. 'I don't even know for sure that it was Ben,' I say. 'And anyway, it's too late. Everyone's already seen the pictures. My life is over, no matter what happens.'

'Look, Midge,' says George. 'Nobody thinks that it's actually *your* body.'

I wonder if I should be insulted by this comment, but I ignore it and walk on. It's really raining now. I wish George and his stupid long eyelashes would leave me alone.

'That's not actually why you're upset, is it?' asks George suddenly.

'What?'

'You're not upset because there're naked pictures of you all over the school.'

'They're not naked pictures of me,' I say.

'Whatever,' says George. 'You're not upset about the fact that there's a rude picture of *you*. You're upset that there's a rude picture of *me*.'

'What are you talking about?' I say. 'Of course I'm upset there're rude pictures of me.'

George shakes his head. 'Not as upset as you are about being in it with me. You don't care if people think you're—' he blushes, '. . . a *harlot* — you just don't want them to think that we're going out. You and me.'

'We're not going out,' I say hastily.

'I'm aware of that, Midge.'

George aims a savage kick at an empty take-away coffee cup.

'What's so wrong with me, anyway?' says George.

The coffee cup bounces into the gutter and then rolls out onto the road.

'Am I that odious to you?'

I know he's looking right at me, but I keep my eyes on the coffee cup. A car whooshes past and flattens it.

'Would it really harm your precious reputation so much to be seen with me?'

I think about Tahni, lying on my bed, crying with laughter as she described George in his suit of armour. I think about the way he jiggles when he runs. I think about the way he wears his school shorts. I bite my lip and don't say anything.

George stops walking. 'You're unbelievable,' he says. 'I thought you were different, but you're just as shallow as all the others.'

I march on. I start to cry again, but I pretend it's just the rain.

## 14  **scourge**

/skɜrdʒ/

–noun; 1.  a whip or lash, esp. for the infliction of
             punishment or torture.
         2.  a cause of affliction or calamity.

– The Wordsmith's Dictionary of Hard-to-spell Words

Mum and Dad are waiting for me when I get home. They're sitting at the table with cups of tea. I'm surprised to see Mum, because I thought she was still away with work.

'Are you okay, sweetheart?' asks Mum. She gets up and hugs me. She smells different. New perfume.

I resist the urge to burst into tears. Instead, I sniff and nod.

'Who would do something like that?' Dad asks.

I shrug. How can I tell them? They don't even know about Ben.

'How is your friend?' asks Mum. 'The other one in . . . in the pictures.'

'He's not my friend,' I say. 'Just someone I'm doing an assignment with.'

Mum pours me a cup of tea.

'Is there anything you want to tell us, Midge?' asks Mum.

'No,' I say in a very quiet voice, looking down at my mug. Doesn't Mum remember I hate tea?

'Because you know you can talk to us about anything,' she says. 'No matter what it is.'

'There's nothing,' I say. 'I don't know why it happened. I don't know why I was chosen. They probably just opened up the school roll and threw a pin at a name.'

Why is Dad being so quiet? This is normally the part where he makes a stupid joke to lighten the mood. Or gets furious that someone defiled his daughter's name and stamps around the house yelling. But he's just sitting there, staring at his hands.

Now what? Are they waiting for me to speak? Do they think that this understanding, tea-drinking family time will lead to me spilling out the truth about Ben and Tahni and George and how I'm an idiot and have no friends left in the world and am going to end up a lonely old lady with eleven cats much sooner than I imagined? Not likely.

'Anyway,' says Mum. 'It's good that we have this chance to all sit down together.'

Huh? We live together. We sit down together for dinner every night. Although we haven't been doing that much lately. Still.

'Midge,' says Mum. 'We need to talk.'

Oh. Is this where they finally tell me Grandma died?

She glances at Dad, but he's staring down at his mug. His face looks funny.

'Midge . . .' says Mum again, and then trails off.

'What is it?' I say.

Now Mum looks down at her cup of tea. I think she might be crying.

I suddenly get the feeling that this isn't about Grandma. Mum and Dad aren't making eye contact. What's going on? Is someone dying? Does Dad have cancer? Are we bankrupt? Is Mum a drug dealer? Is she going to goal? Am I adopted? Does Dad have a secret love-child? Or a whole other family? Are they going back to Russia to be with Svetlana? Or are they time-travellers from the future? Or terrorists?

'Your mother's having an affair.'

Dad says it shortly, abruptly, without glancing up from his cup of tea.

'What?'

Mum closes her eyes. 'I'm sorry, Midge,' she says.

I must have heard wrong.

'Tell her,' says Dad.

Mum sighs. 'You know I work very long hours, Midge,' she says. 'And so I've been spending a lot of time with Jason. And being a lawyer is so intense. And it just . . .'

'Jason?' I say. 'You had an affair with a lawyer called Jason?'

Mum nods.

I think about the long hours she's been working. Working late on a Saturday night and 'falling asleep at her desk'. I remember the fancy roast dinner she cooked, and all the things she bought me on our girls' day out. It was guilt. It wasn't about me at all. It was about *Jason*.

'When did it start?' I ask.

'About six months ago,' says Mum.

Dad's hands are wrapped around his mug. His knuckles are white. I imagine someone else's hands touching my Mum. I imagine her kissing another man. I feel sick and shivery and very, very wrong. The smell of Mum's new perfume is overpowering.

'But it's over now, right?' I say.

Mum squirms. I think Dad's stopped breathing. 'No, sweetheart,' she says. 'It's not over.'

'Why not?' I ask.

'Because I'm not sure what I want,' she says.

I'm sorry, but isn't it the *dad* who's supposed to have the affair? He's supposed to turn forty or fifty and get a red sports car and have an affair with a twenty-five-year-old leggy blonde. That's how it happens on television. The mother *never* has the affair.

'Are you getting a divorce?' I ask.

'I'm going to go and stay with a friend for a while,' says Mum. Her voice is squeaky. 'While we figure things out.'

'A *friend*?' I say, with a healthy amount of sarcasm.

'Yes,' she says. 'Just a girlfriend.'

I swallow.

'Midge,' says Mum, and I wonder why she keeps saying my name. It's as though she thinks she's going to forget it or something. She might. 'Midge, I want you to know that no matter what happens, I'll always be your mum. You're always my number one priority.'

'Oh please,' I say. 'If I was your number one priority, you'd keep our family together. You wouldn't have run out and slept with the first bloke you met like a *harlot*.'

'Don't talk to your mother that way,' says Dad.

I look at him, and feel panic. How can I live with just Dad? He can't cook, and he doesn't know how to sew up the hem of my school uniform, and he won't know when I have to go to the dentist or remember that I don't like mushrooms or tea.

I can't handle this. It's all Mum's fault. I stand up. 'She's not my mother.'

I walk out. I just want to go to my room and cry on my bed, but that doesn't feel dramatic enough. So I walk out the front door.

Why couldn't Mum have been the one with the imaginary boyfriend?

## 15  venge·ance

/ˈvɛndʒəns/

–noun; infliction of injury, harm, humiliation,
or the like, on a person by another who has
been harmed by that person.

– The Wordsmith's Dictionary of Hard-to-spell Words

It's still raining outside. Everything is grey and miserable. I run out of the front gate and stand on the footpath, under the shelter of a wattle tree.

I am totally numb. How could Mum do this? On today of all days? What did I do to the universe to deserve this?

Maybe I've just been given all the bad days for the rest of my life in one hit. Maybe this is it – from now on, everything will be puppies and sunshine and daisies. I doubt it.

I find my mobile and call Tahni. I know we've been fighting, but this is bigger than that. I need her.

'Hello?'

'It's me.' My voice is wobbly.

Silence.

'Tahni?' I say.

'I can't talk right now,' she says. She sounds weird.

'But I really need to—'

'See you later,' she says, and hangs up.

I have an urge to throw my phone across the street. I want to smash it against something and see it explode into tiny pieces. I want to break something.

But I put it back in my pocket.

I think about going back inside, but I don't want to see Mum at the moment. Or Dad. I just can't handle it. And Tahni is blowing me off.

So I go to the one place I have left.

A woman answers the door. She must be George's mum. She's quite dumpy, with thick salt-and-pepper hair tied back into a bun. She's wearing a floral dress, with an apron over the top.

'Hi,' I say. 'I'm Midge. I'm George's—. Is George here?'

She smiles at me.

'Welcome,' she says. She has an accent.

She turns and yells, 'Giorgos!' It sounds like *Your-goss*. That must be George's name in Greek.

George yells something from another room. It's not in English. His mum replies with a string of words I absolutely do not understand. Then she switches to English.

'Your friend from school,' she yells. 'Midge. She's a very pretty girl.'

She winks at me. I blush. I don't think I look very pretty right now, all wet and tear-stained and blotchy.

'Come into the kitchen,' she says. 'Giorgos will be down in a minute.'

I follow her into the house. It's quite a big house – bigger than ours, with lots of nice old-fashioned furniture. There are delicate china ornaments on every available surface – cats and lambs and bells and shepherdesses.

Mrs Papadopoulos is a force of nature. Before I'm aware of it, she's got me sitting at the kitchen bench, with a towel around my shoulders, sipping a cup of strong, black coffee and eating a crescent-shaped biscuit dusted with icing sugar. As soon as I bite into the crumbly biscuit, I realise it's what I've been smelling on George. Nutty and sweet and a little bit spicy. The biscuit crumbles and then melts in my mouth. It's delicious, and I help myself to another before I realise what I'm doing.

There's a stew or soup of some kind bubbling away on the stove. The windows are steamed up from the warmth, but I can still see the rain pounding away outside. I feel incredibly comfortable and safe.

This is a *real* kitchen. It has real food cooking in it. Not guilt-food. Mrs Papadopoulos bustles about, stirring the pot, topping up my coffee, asking me if I need a fresh towel, or if I would like to take a shower to warm up. She's a real mum. Not like my mum.

I want to stay in Mrs Papadopoulos's kitchen forever.

George comes into the room. He's sort of rumpled, and his T-shirt is on inside-out. I wonder if he just got dressed.

Mrs Papadopoulos says something in Greek, and then leaves the room.

'Hey,' says George awkwardly, still standing by the door.

'Hey,' I reply. I suddenly remember our fight earlier today (was it really today? I feel like I've aged about a zillion years in the last three hours), and how he had said that I was just as shallow as everyone else.

'Sorry about my mum,' says George. 'She can be a bit full-on.'

'She's awesome,' I say. 'I wish she was my mum.'

A tear slides down m cheek and suddenly I'm sobbing, which is really embarrassing. It's all the more embarrassing because it's obviously freaking George out. He doesn't try to comfort me or even sit down. He just shifts uncomfortably from foot to foot and stares at his shoes.

'I'm sorry,' I say, sniffing. 'I didn't know where else to go. My mum just told me she's having an affair.'

'Oh.' He looks even more uncomfortable. 'I'm sorry to hear that.'

He must still be angry with me. I can't blame him. I wipe my eyes and nose on a corner of the towel, and try to put on a bright face.

'Anyway, I just needed to get out of the house, and I thought we could do some work on our project. We have to give our presentation next week.'

'Right,' says George. 'Only I don't have time. I kind of . . . have this thing tonight. And I have to get ready.'

I frown. 'It's not even lunchtime,' I say. 'What do you have to do that will take so long?'

'Nothing important.'

George bites his lip and I suddenly remember what Tahni

told me. He's going out to do something weird. Something that involves wearing armour. Oh! Is that why he looks like he just got dressed? Because he was trying on his *armour*? Tahni was right. He *is* crazy. He's like a cross between Don Quixote and Saint George. Don George. I giggle, and he raises an eyebrow.

'Are you okay?' he says.

I nod, swallowing a real laugh. Is this what hysteria feels like?

He looks so uncomfortable. I almost tell him that I know his secret, but he'd be so embarrassed and I don't want to make him feel bad. I'm feeling bad enough for both of us. So I stand, and fold the damp towel.

'I'd better be getting home,' I say.

'Okay,' he says. And then, 'It's better that you know.'

'What?'

'About your mum. It's always better to know the truth.'

I think about it. 'No,' I say. 'I'd rather she had kept lying to me about it.'

George shakes his head. 'My dad left when I was three,' he says. 'He just walked out one day. Didn't say anything to anyone, not even Mum. I never knew why.' He smiles at me. 'At least your mum had the guts to tell you.'

I put the towel down on the chair and start to walk out of the kitchen. But I stop before I get to the door.

'Why did you leave your old school?' I ask.

'I did something stupid,' he says. 'I'm an easy target. Someone . . . found out something about me, he spread it all over the school, and everyone picked on me. I thought that revenge was the best way to stop it. I did something . . . something stupid, and we both got expelled.'

So that's why he's so cagey about his dressing-up habit. I wonder what he did, but it's clear he's not going to talk about it.

'We've got lots more secrets,' he says. 'If you could put them together into the visual presentation, I'll write the text.'

I nod. 'Say thanks to your mum for the coffee and the biscuits.'

I walk out of the house, thinking about George and Ben and Tahni. I think about the pictures of me and George, all over the school. And my mind is buzzing with one word, over and over again.

The word sticks with me all week, ringing like a bell.

I take Tuesday off, but go back to school on Wednesday. They've fixed the computers, but everyone still giggles and nudges when I walk past. I don't care. All I care about is the word echoing in my mind.

*Revenge.*

When the final bell rings on Friday afternoon, I pull out my mobile phone and send Ben a text message:

**I'll do your project.**

He texts back in seconds, asking to see what I have so far.

At home, I go straight up to my room. I switch on my

computer and email Ben my proposal and notes for his project. Then I check the Secret Project website and I read through the new secrets.

*I'm scared no one will ever love me.*

*More than anything, I want to take my best friend to the formal. But I'm afraid if I ask her, she'll laugh at me.*

*I really, really like* Star Trek.

*I saw Ms Aitken's undies. They were red.*

*Remember when I let you copy my Chemistry exam, and I got an A+ and you got a C? Well I gave you the wrong answers. Serves you right for cheating.*

*I am always watching you.*

*I think Mr Moss is a zombie. Yesterday, I was walking past his office and I heard him say 'braiiiiiiins'.*

*I'm in love with my best freind's boyfreind, and it makes me hate her.*

*My dad says I'm too fat to play football.*

*On the inside, I'm a hero. But outside, nobody even sees me.*

They make me feel better. Some of them are funny, others are sad, others are a bit scary. Over one hundred secrets have been submitted. So many secrets. I think about the crowded hall at school, full of people who are full of secrets. I imagine all their secrets floating up above them and swirling around together, filling the air with clouds of different coloured secret swirls.

I remember what George said when he first told me about the idea.

*Just the act of writing it down and posting it makes people feel better.*

So I write my own secret, and upload it onto the site.

Then I select my favourites, and set about turning them into a presentation.

## 16 **di·vul·ge**

/dɪˈvʌldʒ/

–verb; to disclose or reveal (something private,
secret, or previously unknown).

– The Wordsmith's Dictionary of Hard-to-spell Words

George and I don't speak much over the next week. He's
still being strange and distant. I think turning up at his
house and blubbering freaked him out even more. He's
clearly uncomfortable around me.

Before I realise, it's Friday. The Friday. The one where we
have to present our projects to the whole year level.

I meet up with Ben before school and give him a folder
of notes and a DVD.

'Did you make the changes I asked for?' he says.

He has been emailing me all week with suggestions. The
amount of time he's spent emailing me, he could have done
his own freaking project.

'I made changes,' I say, carefully.

'It's a bit dry.' Ben flicks through the notes. 'I wanted
something a bit more . . . you know. Sparky.'

I give him my very best sincere smile. 'It's all in the visual presentation,' I tell him. 'There's plenty of sparky on the DVD.'

Ben frowns, and I feel my smile falter. He looks at the DVD in its paper sleeve, and then at the folder of notes.

I stop breathing. He knows. He can see it in my eyes. He's going to snap the DVD in half and throw it on the floor and scream my secret to the whole school. He'll hire a billboard, or one of those blimps that flies around when the football's on. He'll get a sky-writer. He'll rearrange the stars to spell it out so the whole world will know:

MIDGE HAS AN IMAGINARY BOYFRIEND. WHAT A LOOSER.

(I may be a loser, but at least I'm not the one who made an intergalactic spelling mistake.)

Ben doesn't do any of these things. Instead, he shrugs, tucks the folder and the DVD into his bag.

'See you later,' he says.


Chris Stitz is on stage with Josh Nelson, talking about their project to catalogue the various ways you can kill someone in the Manhunt2 videogame. There are lots of very violent pictures. Everyone cheers when they show one character yanking out the spinal cord of another. The teachers are less than enthusiastic. Chris and Josh finish up, to wild applause.

We're next.

The Secret Project was a runaway success. George has written a great report, and I've made the visual presentation.

Hopefully they'll match up, because we haven't been over it together.

'Are you ready?' George asks.

I nod.

He turns and walks towards the stage.

'George—' I say.

He stops.

'I just wanted to say thanks,' I say. 'You made me think a lot. After what you said last week.'

He frowns. 'What did I say?'

'About revenge. About how it's the best way to take action.'

'What?'

I smile. 'Don't worry,' I say. 'It won't affect our presentation.'

'I didn't say that,' he says. 'I never said that revenge was a good thing. I said it was stupid.'

Did he? I don't remember that bit.

'Midge, what won't affect our presentation? What are you going to do?'

'Never mind,' I say. 'I'm just releasing another secret.'

George looks worried, and shakes his head. Then he says something in Greek.

'What's that mean?' I ask.

'It's a proverb,' he explains. 'The tree of revenge yields no fruit.'

'Like you said, it's always better to know the truth,' I say. 'I'm sick of secrets.'

Our presentation goes without a hitch. It's perfect. The teachers love it, the students love it. When I display the secrets, everyone tries to figure out who wrote which ones. Our applause is maybe not as wild as the cheering for the Manhunt2 presentation, but I have a sneaking feeling that we're going to get a better mark.

George's face is pink with pleasure as we walk off the stage.

'That was great!' I say.

He nods, smiling. 'Well done,' he says.

'Well done you,' I reply. 'It was your idea.'

I hear Ben's name called, and I stiffen. He saunters past and winks at me. George raises his eyebrows.

'What did you do?' he asks.

'Shh,' I say. 'Just watch.'

Ben loads the DVD into the laptop, and the presentation launches on the big screen behind him. It's called Photo-Manipulation in the Media: A Case Study. It's impressive, and I'm quite proud.

'I'm presenting a step-by-step analysis of exactly how to create images and animations for movies and magazines,' says Ben, reading from the sheet of paper I gave him. 'I've compiled some before and after shots, to demonstrate that the images of beauty we see in the media are highly manipulated, creating false expectations of what is considered beautiful by readers, particularly young women.'

There's a titter in the auditorium, and Ben looks a little

uncertain. But the image on the screen has clicked over to the next one. I smile, and nod reassuringly.

'Er,' says Ben. 'I've created an example of this manipulation, by taking photos of two ordinary people . . .'

Behind him, the screen wipes to reveal two photos. One of me. And one of George.

The auditorium suddenly goes very quiet. George looks at me, horrified. Ben is still reading, he hasn't seen the images on the screen.

'These images are then disassembled and combined with other images, to create a chimera – an entirely fantastical creature made up of different parts–'

He pronounces *chimera* with a 'ch' sound instead of the correct 'k' sound, which only adds to the heady adrenaline of sweet revenge.

Ben finally looks up at the screen. There's an image on there of various body parts of naked people. He stops talking and his mouth falls open.

The auditorium erupts. Ben punches the keys on the keyboard, but it has no effect. I may not be a computer genius like Tahni, but even I know how to lock a presentation. There's nothing he can do. The pictures continue their animation, assembling themselves into strange naked creatures – with my head on one and George's on the other.

I have to admit that my naked hybrids are not nearly as good as the ones plastered all over the school, and my animation skills are not that great.

Ben is still desperately stabbing keys. George turns and walks out.

'George,' I call, and am about to follow him when Mr Moss climbs the stairs to the stage and quickly removes all the plugs from the back of the computer. The screen goes bright blue and empty.

'I think we've seen enough,' says Mr Moss. 'Ben. My office.'

'But I didn't do it,' Ben says. His face is a strange shade of purple.

The shouting and whistling of the students dies down. No one wants to miss a word.

'I'm extremely disappointed, Ben,' says Mr Moss. 'You are a promising student. I had high hopes for you at this school. But I'm afraid a stunt like this can only lead to expulsion.'

A shiver of excitement ripples through the auditorium. It's like a public lynching. Or a witch-burning.

'But I didn't do it. I didn't.' Ben turns to me. 'Midge,' he says.

There is a murmur in the crowd as everyone cranes their necks to see me, standing just off-stage.

'Midge, tell them I didn't do it.'

I walk onto the stage. My knees are trembling. The word is still thumping away in my head. Revenge. Revenge. Revenge. I think of every single cruel, manipulative, careless thing Ben ever said to me. I want him to suffer. I want him to be humiliated.

But there's something else in my head. Something else is repeating over and over again. It's not as loud as the revenge drums, but I can still hear it.

It's George's voice, talking about my mum. *It's always better to know the truth.*

Is it though? Is it really? If Mum hadn't told me about her affair, then I wouldn't be so upset. And Dad wouldn't be so upset. Surely that would be better.

But we would have found out eventually.

Everyone is still staring at me. I step forward onto the stage.

'No,' I say. 'He didn't do it.'

Mr Moss frowns at me. 'How do you know, Imogen?'

I swallow. 'Because I made his presentation for him. He's never seen it before today.'

The tittering and whispering all stops. I can hear myself breathing. Inhale. Exhale.

'I made the presentation,' I say. 'Ben made me do his project for him.'

Mr Moss glares at Ben again, and I sigh.

'I made up an imaginary boyfriend,' I say. 'At the beginning of term. Because I was sick of everyone telling me how pathetic I was. I was sick of being embarrassed that I'd never had a boyfriend. So I made one up. His name was Ben, and he was English and he was perfect. I made up all sorts of stuff about him. I even made him a MySpace page. Then one day he turned up here at school.'

The students are all spellbound. For a moment I pretend

I'm sitting down there with them, and there's some other freakazoid chick up here spilling her guts about what a sad losery psycho she is.

'It wasn't my imaginary boyfriend, of course, it was just a coincidence that he was a New Boy called Ben and had an English accent. But everyone thought he was my Ben. And he figured it out, and agreed to go along with it. Except then he wanted me to do his project for him, and I didn't want to. So I told him it was over. And he told me I'd regret it. So when I came to school and saw the pictures of me and George, I thought it was him. I wanted revenge, so I told him I'd changed my mind and would do his project. And I made this.'

'So Ben *is* responsible for the lewd pictures?' asks Mr Moss.

'No,' I say. 'He didn't do it.'

'But how do you know?' insists Mr Moss.

This is it. I take a deep breath, and stare down into the audience, at my best friend in the whole world.

'Because Tahni did it,' I say.

# 17 e·piph·a·ny
/əˈpɪfəni/

–noun; a sudden, intuitive perception of or insight
    into the reality or essential meaning of
    something.

*– The Wordsmith's Dictionary of Hard-to-spell Words*

I'm in Mr Moss's office.

After my rather dramatic declaration of Tahni's guilt,
Tahni burst into tears and ran out of the auditorium, which
pretty much proved she was guilty. Because you know, if
you didn't do it, you'd be sitting there saying, 'I didn't do it!'
And she didn't. So she did do it. Also, she confessed
everything to the school nurse after she vomited into her
locker.

Mr Moss is totally livid.

'Tahni's lewd stunt is a very serious matter,' says Mr Moss.
'I'll be talking to both your parents, and you and George
should think about whether you want them to press
charges.'

I swallow. I don't want to get Tahni into any more
trouble. I wonder what George will do.

'Shouldn't George be here too?' I ask.

'He had to leave early,' says Mr Moss.

'Leave?' I say. 'To go where?'

'I don't know, Imogen,' he says. 'He had a note from his mother excusing him from afternoon classes.'

Maybe he's off slaying a dragon or rescuing some maiden in distress. I wish he was here. I could use some rescuing right now.

'I'm suspending Ben Wheeler for the rest of term,' Mr Moss continues.

I swallow. This is the part where I get handed out my punishment.

'I'm tempted to suspend you too, Imogen,' he says. 'But apart from having a rather overactive imagination, and exposing the wrongdoings of your classmates, you don't seem to have done anything wrong.'

'What about Ben's project?' I ask, while silently telling myself to shut up in case Mr Moss changes his mind. The last thing I need is to be suspended. Then I'd have to spend more time at home, which is something I absolutely do not want to be doing right now.

Mr Moss scratches his head. A few dandruff flakes drift onto the shoulders of his suit-jacket. 'What you did was unbelievably stupid,' he says. 'Agreeing to do Ben's home-work for him in exchange for him pretending to be your boyfriend was undignified and foolish, and gives me serious cause for concern about your sense of self-respect. What's more, attempting to expose him for a crime he didn't commit in front of the whole school was inappropriate and incredibly immature. I hope that in the future, you will exercise a little more wisdom in your conduct, Imogen.' He sighs. 'However, I'm willing to concede that between the lewd pictures, the extra work you've done to cover for Ben, and the judgement of your classmates, you've been punished enough.'

I nod, swallowing. He's got a point.

'Unless you would like to spend some time away from school,' Mr Moss adds. 'I can suspend you if you want some time to contemplate your actions.'

'No,' I say, hurriedly. 'I'm fine. And I don't want to press charges.'

Mr Moss nods, and makes a note. 'Thank you, Imogen,' he says. 'Could you please send Tahni in on your way out?'

Tahni is sitting outside Mr Moss's office. Her face is red and blotchy.

She looks up at me and everything is Awkward.

'Mr Moss wants you now,' I say.

'How did you know it was me?' Tahni asks.

I shrug. 'You spelt 'friends' wrong on your secret.'

She looks at me, blankly.

'*I'm in love with my best freind's boyfreind, and it makes me hate her.* You spelt "friend" wrong. Twice.'

Tahni raises her eyebrows. 'What are you, Nancy Drew?'

'There were other things as well. The way you flirted with Ben. How you hate George so much.'

She bites her lip. 'I'm sorry,' she says. 'You looked so happy. I wanted that. Everything is always so easy for you.'

'You think?' I say. 'I made up an imaginary boyfriend, my real boyfriend was just as fake, I revealed both of those things to the entire school, and my best friend hates me. Oh, and did I mention my mother is having an affair?'

'I'm sorry,' Tahni says again.

'That's okay,' I say. 'You can't help who you fall in love with.'

As I say it, I realise how true it is. I sigh. This isn't going to be easy.

'Well,' says Tahni, standing up. 'I'd better go.'

I nod.

'See ya,' she says.

'Hey,' I say. 'Can I ask you something?'

'Sure.'

'Why didn't you tell anyone you knew about me and Ben and the whole imaginary boyfriend thing?'

Tahni frowns. 'I didn't know,' she says.

'Then who was listening at the door when I told Ben I wasn't doing his project any more?'

'It wasn't me,' says Tahni. 'If I'd known, things probably would have been much worse.'


I go home and climb straight into bed. I really, really want to fall asleep and forget that the last few weeks ever happened. I can't even think about Mum and Dad, or Tahni, or Ben and the horrible pictures of me and George. In fact, all I can think about is how horrified George was when he saw the presentation I'd made for Ben. And how he looked when I told him about getting revenge. I don't know why I care what he thinks of me; after all, he's the guy who wears the school shorts, and dresses up like a knight and tries to kill dragons. But I do. I hate the thought that he's disappointed in me.

I have never been so glad to wake up and realise it's Saturday. When I finally crawl out of bed, I find Mum sitting at the kitchen table. She's wearing a jumper I haven't seen before, and jeans. I haven't seen my mother wear jeans in . . . well, ever.

I don't want to see her.

'What are you doing here?' I ask. 'Where's Dad?'

'He's gone to see your grandma,' says Mum. 'And I came to see you.'

I open the fridge, but there's nothing in there except for sad bendy vegetables and milk that passed its use-by date about a week ago.

'Mr Moss called me,' says Mum.

I suppose now I get a Lecture. I don't say anything.

'I'm not unaware of the irony here,' says Mum. 'You pretend to have a boyfriend when you don't. I pretend not to have a boyfriend when I do.'

'Wanna swap?' I ask. I don't look at her.

Mum sighs. 'I should punish you,' she says. 'What you did was really, really dumb. And you should have talked to me about it. But I realise I haven't been very available lately. And I know things have been difficult for you this term. With everything.'

I sit down at the kitchen table.

'And I think it would be hypocritical of me to ground you.'

She's right. It would be totally hypocritical.

'So,' she says, smiling. 'Just make sure you keep your imaginary friends strictly platonic from now on.'

I don't smile back. 'Does that go for you too?' I ask.

Mum looks serious all of a sudden. 'That's why I wanted to talk to you,' she says.

This is it. This is where she tells me she's moving in with Jason and I will never see her again and she's going to buy a sports car and Dad will become an alcoholic and I will officially be a child from a Broken Home.

'I'm not seeing Jason anymore,' she says. 'We broke up.'

I hold my breath. Really? The affair is over? She can come home, and be normal and cook tofu burgers and nutloaf and I will eat it happily. (Or at least pretend to.)

'So you're coming home?' I ask.

She takes a deep breath. 'No,' she says. 'I'm not.'

I don't think I can handle living on this emotional roller-coaster. I want to get off.

'I need to figure some stuff out,' says Mum. 'Things are clearly not working between your father and me.'

'Because you were having an affair,' I say. 'Now you're not.'

'I had the affair because I was unhappy,' says Mum.

'Why?' I ask, starting to cry. I feel like a five year old. 'Why were you unhappy?'

Was it me?

'Sweetheart, I don't know,' she says. 'That's what I need to figure out. I need to figure out who *I* am. What *I* want.'

'What about what *I* want?' I say, my voice shaking. 'What about what Dad wants?'

Mum bites her lip. 'You don't want this,' she says. 'You know you don't.'

She's right. I don't want the secrets and the whispering and the fake family dinners. I don't want to come down to the kitchen in the middle of the night to find my father crying at the kitchen table.

'But I don't want you to go,' I say.

Mum starts to cry too, and she gets up to hug me. 'Neither do I,' she says.

I bury my head in her new jumper. She still smells different.

'So *don't*,' I say.

But I know she has to. I hug her as tightly as I can and we cry. If this were a TV show, I'd tell her how much I love her, and she'd tell me that she was *so proud* of me. But it isn't, so we don't.

After a while, things feel a bit less insane, I make tea (black, because I don't trust the milk) and we sit and drink it together. I still don't like it, but it feels like the right thing to do so I try not to screw up my face as I sip it.

'So,' I say, stirring sugar into my tea. 'Does this mean I get twice as many Christmas presents?'

Mum laughs. 'Sure,' she says. 'But half of them will be imaginary.'

'I think I'll pass,' I say. 'I've had enough of imaginary for a while.'

'There's nothing wrong with imaginary,' says Mum. 'Imaginary is good. Just don't take it too far.'

I nod.

'Did you really feel that bad you didn't have a boyfriend?' says Mum. 'Did people give you a hard time about it?'

I nod again and bite my lip. 'I just wanted to be a normal girl.'

Mum gives my arm a squeeze. 'You're an amazing girl,' she says. 'And you have the rest of your life to find the perfect boyfriend. Any day now they'll be lining up at your door.'

I snort. 'Not after the stunt I pulled today, they won't.'

'The right one won't care,' says Mum. 'He will love you for your brilliant imagination.'

'I won't hold my breath,' I say.

'Just be patient,' says Mum. 'Your knight in shining armour will turn up one day.'

We talk for a bit longer, then Mum gets up and carries our mugs over to the sink. She rinses them, and I dry with the last clean tea towel.

'I'm going to start looking for an apartment tomorrow,' she says. 'Do you want to help?'

'Sure,' I reply.

She kisses me on the cheek and hugs me once more. Then she swings her bag over her shoulder and perches her sunglasses on her head. She actually looks pretty good in those jeans.

'Mum, wait!' I yell, and follow her down the corridor. She's standing by the front door.

'What is it?' she asks.

'You're wrong,' I tell her. 'About being patient. About waiting for my knight in shining armour to turn up.'

Mum raises an eyebrow. 'What?'

I laugh. 'Don't worry,' I say. 'I'll see you tomorrow.'

She shakes her head, smiling, and walks out the door.

## 18 **par·rhe·si·a**

/ˈpərɪʒə/

–noun; freedom or boldness of speech:
outspokenness.

– The Wordsmith's Dictionary of Hard-to-spell Words

George's mother opens the door. She's wearing a different apron, and she's carrying a wooden spoon. The biscuity smell is stronger than ever and makes me hungry and happy and nervous all at the same time.

'Ah! Giorgos's friend,' she says, smiling broadly.

'Hi, Mrs Papadopoulos,' I say. I'm about to ask her if George is home, but it doesn't quite happen, and before I know it, I'm sitting at her kitchen table again, drinking thick black coffee and eating crescent moon biscuits. Not that I'm complaining. The biscuits are good, really good.

'Um, is George home?' I ask, after my third biscuit. I feel a bit stupid for waiting so long to ask.

'No,' says Mrs Papadopoulos. 'He is out all day today.'

I bite my lip. 'Do you know where I can find him? I really need to talk to him.'

Mrs Papadopoulos shakes her head. 'Sorry, *matia mou*.'

'You don't know? Or you're not going to tell me?'

'Giorgos is busy today. He has a special hobby and he is very dedicated. But he doesn't like me to boast about his hobby.'

'But why not?'

She opens the oven and the delicious, garlicky smell nearly knocks me to the floor. 'Some people, they don't understand. They make fun of my Giorgos.'

'I do,' I tell her. 'I totally understand.'

She shakes her head again.

'Please, Mrs Papadopoulos,' I say. 'I need to see George. I need to tell him something. It's important.'

She is bent over the open oven, but she turns her head and looks up at me. I can tell she's considering it.

'Please,' I say. 'I did something stupid. Actually, I did a whole lot of things that were stupid. And I need to apologise to George, and tell him . . .'

I'm not quite sure I can say it in front of his *mother*.

'. . . tell him the truth.' I finish lamely.

She closes the oven door and stands up.

'You're a very pretty girl,' she says. 'My Giorgos is special.'

'I know,' I tell her. 'That's why I need to talk to him.'

She nods. 'He has a class,' she says. 'In the city.'

She writes down the address. Her handwriting is exactly the same as George's.

'Thank you,' I say, standing up. 'And thanks for the coffee. Your biscuits are amazing.'

I catch a train into the city. It's busy, with lots of people running around with shopping bags and pointy elbows. Everyone seems to be in a hurry, even the people sitting outside cafés seem to be chugging down espressos like it's a race to see who can consume the most caffeine in under a minute.

The address Mrs Papadopoulos gave me turns out to be a building in the financial district. It's one of those old art-deco buildings with a crazy lift that's operated by a real person and has a cage door that rattles and clangs closed before the lift can go up or down. The foyer is musty and dimly lit — it feels like a movie set. I check the information board that lists the building's occupants. I don't even know what I'm looking for. There're so many strange names — the Victorian Spiritualist Investigator's League, Kanzen Kimono Fabrics & Accessories, the Australia China Friendship Society, Buttonmania, University of the Third Age — it could be any of them.

I consider the possibility of the Victorian Drama Association, then I see: L8 LARP Battle Workshop Training Hall, and I get a strange trembling feeling in my stomach. Although that might just be from Mrs Papadopoulos's coffee.

I press the call button for the lift. Nothing happens for a moment, then there's a terrible clanking and groaning noise, and a good five minutes later, the lift arrives.

The operator is a middle-aged man with a ginger beard perched on a high stool. He wears a proper bellboy hat, and a Sex Pistols T-shirt. The walls of the lift are covered in flyers and photos and ticket stubs.

'Buttons?' he says.

I blink. 'I beg your pardon?'

'Are you here for buttons?' he says. 'Most young ladies are.'

'Um, no,' I reply. 'Level eight, please.'

He nods, and cranks the big metal lever. The lift shutters and squeals, and we slowly start to rise. I wonder if I will get out of here alive.

'Frockfairies,' says the ginger man suddenly.

'Sorry?'

He shakes his head. 'Fan Fiction Writers of Victoria? Lupus Australia Association? Not the Asbestos Information Service?'

'No,' I say. 'I'm going to the Battle Workshop Training Hall.'

Ginger raises his eyebrows, then looks me up and down, taking in my jeans and T-shirt.

'Interesting,' he says. 'I wouldn't have picked that. Not in a million years.'

Which is about how long this lift ride is taking.

'You're a Larper?' he asks, a suspicious edge to his tone.

'No,' I say, although I have no idea what a Larper is, and could well be one without knowing. I doubt it though. It sounds like a disease. 'I'm just looking for someone.'

He frowns. 'I don't like your chances today,' he says. 'It's dead quiet up there.'

Good. George and I will have some privacy.

'Looking for your boyfriend?'

What is he, a mind-reader? 'Um, sort of.'

Ginger nods. 'Right. Not your boyfriend yet. You need to tell him how you feel. An *Ain't no Mountain High Enough* moment.'

I stare at him. Is he crazy?

'Like in *Bridget Jones*,' he explains. 'Where she runs through the snow with no pants on to tell Mr Darcy she loves him.'

Okay. Now I'm terrified. I'm trapped in a small metal cage of dubious construction, with a ginger-bearded, Bridget-Jones-loving mind-reader. I want to get out now.

'Make sure you've got the right person,' Ginger says. 'It's hard to tell with that lot, once they've got their gear on. And while a hilarious mistaken-identity moment would be a great beginning for a romantic comedy of errors, I suspect you'd rather that this was the end of the movie, not the beginning.'

I wish this was the end of this elevator-ride, I can tell you that much.

The lift finally squeals to a halt, and Ginger pulls the wire cage door open. 'Good luck,' he says.

When I step out into the corridor, I know something is amiss. Mostly because the lights are off, and it's pitch black. I turn to ask Ginger if I'm on the right floor, but the lift has already sunk down out of sight with suspicious speed and silence.

I can't see a thing. I grope my way forward, and feel wood panelling. A wall. Good start. I feel along the wall, until I reach a door. I try the handle, but it's locked. I keep going. The third door I come to opens. There must be a window somewhere in the room, because dim light vaguely illuminates strange shapes lining the walls. Suits of armour. My heart beats faster. I'm in the right place.

I finally locate a light switch, and flick it. The fluorescent lights *plink* on, and I have to close my eyes for a moment, because it's so bright.

When I open them, I keep blinking to make sure what I see is real. There are racks of armour on one wall. An armoury of swords and spears and other weapons on another. A huge banner hangs over them. It says *LARP Battle Workshop Training Hall*. It smells dusty and sweaty, a bit like the gym at school.

But there's no one here. No George. No knights. No dragons. No anyone.

So much for my *Ain't No Mountain High Enough* moment. I switch off the light, and fumble my way back to the lift.

'No luck?' says Ginger.

I shake my head. Typical. This is just typical. I go for the grand gesture, and what do I get? Nothing. A lift-ride with a crazy redhead.

'Oh well,' says Ginger. 'Plenty more armour-plated fantasists in the sea.'

The lift rattles and shakes down to the ground floor, and

I try not to cry. Ginger hops off his stool and drags the lift door open.

'Hey,' he says, ripping a flyer down from the wall and handing it to me. 'Say hi to Mr Darcy for me.'

On the flyer is a picture of a knight holding a sword, and a wizard with a staff. I recognise the drawings – they're just like the ones George doodles at school.

## 19 **con·quest**

/ˈkɒnˌkwest/

–noun; the overcoming of a problem or weakness

–a person whose affection has been won.

– The Wordsmith's Dictionary of Hard-to-spell Words

The train takes forever to get to Diamond Valley. I feel like I must be at the edge of the universe (I hope the universe is in a good mood, we haven't exactly been getting on lately).

A huge banner hangs above the carpark outside the Diamond Valley Football Oval. It reads *Neverquest: the Ultimate Battle.* I take a deep breath.

The Diamond Valley Football Oval is teeming with . . . I want to say weirdos, but here, in my jeans and T-shirt – I'm the weirdo. There're about a hundred people, dressed in the strangest outfits I've ever seen. Knights and wizards and princesses and . . . other strange creatures that might be orcs.

There are plenty of Gandalf/Dumbledore look-alikes, with pointy hats and flowing cloaks that are muddy around the hem. Two wizards are holding hands. The words *Wizard Love: Out and Proud* are embroidered in silver on their cloaks.

I grin, but then I notice one of them is wearing Nikes underneath his cloak, and am strangely disappointed.

A few outfits are simply woeful. Knitted jumpers spray-painted silver to look like chain mail, teamed with tracksuit pants. Over this is what I can only guess is supposed to be armour, but it looks so totally and utterly lame that I can't believe they're allowed to join in. It looks like cardboard. One guy is wearing a cape that's just a piece of cheap leopard-print fabric, and has decorated his shield with an airbrush fantasy picture of a snow leopard. I feel really sorry for these guys. I mean, if they can't fit in *here*, there isn't much hope for them.

A gaggle of women congregate around a Mr Whippy ice-cream van. They're wearing long flowing medieval dresses with drooping sleeves and silly hats. Some costumes are amazing, with intricate gold embroidery and little pearls and feathers. Others look like they came straight from the bargain basement at a discount fabric store.

There are some women in combat costume as well. A little troupe of girls my age are dressed in Robin Hood-style outfits, with bows and arrows and tights and pointy boots and cute little caps.

Another group of women have blue faces and strange masks made of ivy leaves. They're wearing close-fitting, green dresses and look, frankly, a bit creepy.

An old guy walks past me. He's brandishing a sword that is seriously as big as he is. I'm sure it can't be made out of metal, or else he wouldn't be able to wave it around like he is.

'G'day,' he says to me with a nod.

I smile weakly.

A temporary pavilion in the middle of the oval is decorated with colourful banners and ribbons. In front of it a big crowd of people are watching a fight between what appears to be a ninja and a troll. I perch on a park bench just outside the oval fence and watch too. Ninja (I'm not sure if it's male or female) is dressed from head to toe in tight-fitting black leather – even his/her face is covered in a black leather mask.

Troll is wearing only a loincloth – although it looks more like a dirty nappy on his pale, spindly frame. He's almost purple with cold. He's carrying an enormous clobbering-stick like the ones in old cartoons where the cave man clobbers the cave woman over the head and drags her back to his cave to have his way with her.

They circle around each other for a while, and then Troll tries to clobber Ninja with his big stick. Ninja ducks easily, and throws a silver disc (which looks suspiciously like a CD) at Troll. It hits him on the thigh, and one of the Gandalfs yells 'Blood!' Everyone applauds.

Troll makes another attack, and whacks Ninja on the head. The clobbering-stick bends, and I realise it must be made out of rubber or foam.

'Blood!' yells the Gandalf again.

Ninja then unleashes what looks like his entire CD collection all over Troll, and the Gandalf yells 'Victory!'

Troll turns to him. 'Dude,' he says. 'Are you serious?'

I can't be certain because of the beard and fake eyebrows, but I think the Gandalf is scowling at Troll.

'Victory!' he repeats sternly.

'Fine, whatever,' says Troll, and falls to the ground, apparently dead, but clearly not happy about it.

'Next!' yells the Gandalf over the applause.

A Bedouin-tiger-man in puffy orange pants and a fully armoured knight step into the ring. The knight's armour, I have to say, is impressive. It's silver and shiny and yet dinted and dirty enough to look like it's seen some serious battle-action. He has an enormous sword (with gaffer tape wrapped around the pointy end), a scary stick with nasty looking spikes on one end, and he exudes confident knightliness.

'Begin!' yells the Gandalf. I wonder if he's capable of speaking in actual full sentences. Maybe that's why he got this job.

Tiger-man has a curvy-sword like the ones from the Aladdin stories. He leaps right into it, slashing at the knight with vigour. But the knight is awesome. He parries and thrusts and does fancy things with his sword. It's a blur. He spins around as if he wasn't wearing about a hundred kilos of metal, and systematically destroys Tiger-man's defences. It feels like it's all over in about ten seconds. The crowd goes wild.

Tiger-man gets up from his death-pose and wanders off sulkily. The knight does a victory air-punch and bows to the crowd. He even stares at me for a moment, then raises a gauntleted hand in a salute, and I wave back. Someone hands him a funny little hat that says 'OOC', and he places it on his helmet.

Then he comes clanking over to me.

He pushes back his visor, and underneath it's George. He's puffing and dirty and his cheeks are flushed and his eyes are all excited and shiny. His eyelashes seem longer than ever.

'Did you see?' he says.

'I saw,' I reply. 'You were amazing. Brave. Chivalrous. True.'

'Really?'

'Well maybe not so much of the chivalrous,' I say. 'The way you smashed him in the head with that pointy-ended stick—'

'It's called a mace,' George says.

'Whatever. That didn't exactly display a whole lot of knightly virtue.'

George shrugs. 'It was fun, though.'

He removes his helmet and sits next to me in a clanking jangle.

'How did you know I was here?' he says.

I pull the flyer out of my pocket, and tell him about his mum and Ginger.

George looks impressed. 'You've had quite an adventure,' he says.

'I needed to talk to you.'

'And you couldn't have called? Knights have mobile phones now, you know.'

'I wanted to talk in person,' I say.

He nods, and we sit for a moment. I haven't really thought about how this conversation would go.

'"OOC"?' I say, pointing at the helmet. 'I'm guessing "Out of Control".'

'"Out of Character",' says George. 'I'm being George now, not my character. You have to let people know, or it gets confusing.'

'So that wasn't George, fighting?' I ask.

'No,' he says. 'It was Sir Andreas of Wurster.'

'Huh,' I say. 'So where is Sir Andreas now?'

'He had some business to take care of,' says George. 'An appointment.'

'With Death?'

'Accountant. Even knights have to pay the bills.'

'Okay,' I say. 'Now is the part where you tell me what's going on.'

'It's LARPing,' he says. 'I'm a LARPer.'

'Which means . . .'

'It stands for Live Action Role-Playing,' George says. 'We have a world and characters and we have battles and alliances and quests. It's sort of like Dungeons and Dragons, or World of Warcraft, but we actually have the courage to leave our bedrooms and *do* stuff. I'm from Wurster, which is purple,' he brushes his hand against the feather in his helmet. 'We're not doing so well at the moment, one of our best knights just got a new job in Canberra, and another is pregnant. So we're low on numbers.'

'But you were really good,' I say. 'You beat that guy with the whiskers and silly pants.'

'I did,' says George. 'But there's only one of me. I'm great one-on-one, but in a battle against fifty Simikk warriors, I'm toast.'

'What happens if they kill you?' I ask.

'I'm not allowed to play for twenty-four hours.'

'Harsh,' I say.

'So,' says George. 'Do you think I'm crazy?'

I look around. 'You spend time in a very weird imaginary world,' I say.

He nods. 'There're some strange people, but it's fun.'

I think about this. I think I'm over my first reaction which was definitely of the 'what a bunch of losers' variety.

'It's pretty impressive,' I say. 'I mean, the cardboard armour guys are kind of lame, but other costumes are awesome. And you've obviously put a lot of practice into all the fighting.'

George makes this cute little bow that is rather hampered by all the metal he's wearing.

'So you don't think I'm a weirdo?' says George.

'Oh,' I tell him. 'You're definitely a weirdo. But if you ask me, golf is a pretty weird hobby too. At least you guys are using your imaginations, and being creative and productive. You can't say that about golf.'

'No, you can't,' says George.

'Or me,' I say, taking a deep breath. 'You can't say that about me either. All this puts my imaginary boyfriend to shame.'

George laughs, but I hear a tiny twinge of nervousness. This makes me feel better, somehow.

'I'm sorry,' I say. 'I'm really, really sorry. About the revenge thing, and calling you a weirdo, and being awful. And I should have told you about Ben. That it wasn't real.'

'That's okay,' George says. 'I already knew.'

'It was you that overheard us,' I say.

He nods.

'Why didn't you say anything?'

'I didn't want to embarrass you,' he says. 'You obviously didn't want to talk about it. Anyway, I was busy keeping my own secrets.'

He raps on his armoured chest.

'Yeah,' I say. 'About that.'

He looks at me, and I grin and shrug. 'You knew?' he says, his forehead crinkling in a truly adorable way. 'How?'

'Tahni was in the hospital bed next to yours.'

He laughs again, and this time there is less nervous twinge. 'We're not very good at this secret thing, are we?'

I think about our project. I think about the secret that I am now sure was George's.

*On the inside, I'm a hero. But outside, nobody even sees me.*

'I see you,' I tell him.

I put my hand on his. It's sheathed in a metal gauntlet, which is not exactly the *Ain't No Mountain High Enough* moment of connection I was going for, but it's enough for now.

He smiles a smile that is shy and embarrassed and a little bit mischievous. 'I have another secret,' he says.

'Really?'

He leans forward and kisses me.

It's not the perfect kiss. It's hard to get close to him with all the armour. His gauntlets are cold and digging into me. And when I put my hands on his shoulders, I get the strange feeling I'm embracing a robot. And even if the armour wasn't there, I know that George doesn't have perfect shoulders underneath the armour.

But it's a *real* kiss. My first real kiss, and it feels perfect.

# Au·thor

/Lili Wilkinson/

–Lili Wilkinson was born in Melbourne, Australia, in the front room where her parents still live. She's an only child, and loves it. She was first published when she was thirteen, in *Voiceworks* magazine. After studying Creative Arts at Melbourne University, Lili was employed by the Centre for Youth Literature at the State Library of Victoria, where she now manages insideadog.com.au, a website for teenagers about books and reading. She spends most of her time reading and writing books for teenagers, but when she's not doing that, she's usually hanging out with friends, watching DVDs and making monsters out of wool.

website: www.liliwilkinson.com
blog: www.liliwilkinson.com/a/blog.html